The

CleanUp

Woman 2:

Bound and Determined

ALISHA YVONNE

Ebony Literary Grace

The CleanUp Woman 2:
Bound and Determined

ALISHA YVONNE

Ebony Literary Grace
PO Box 18080
Memphis, TN 38181-0080

ISBN 10: 0-9746367-7-0
ISBN 13: 978-0-9746367-7-1

Library of Congress Control Number: 2012901426

First Printing: January 2012

Printed in the United States of America

10 9 8 7 6 5 4 3 2 1

This is a work of fiction. Any references or similarities to actual events, real people, living, or dead, or to real locals are intended to give the novel a sense of reality. Any similarity in other names, characters, places, and incidents is entirely coincidental.

Prologue

*T*he sirens were loud. Very loud. In fact, they were almost unbearable as we all ran down the halls toward the exits, trying to escape the intense smoke. Fear claimed every face I could make out clearly in the darkened haze. Doctors, patients, and other staff—they all feared for their lives. But not me. Me—I smirked underneath the small washcloth I used to block the smoke as I breathed. Everyone hurriedly made our way out to the back lawn. Firemen met us just outside the exit.

"Move it, move it," one of them screamed. "Move all the way out now! Get as far from the building as possible."

It was a sight to be seen. More than three hundred people—patients and staff members—all scrambled to the edge of the lawn, which was skirted by dense trees. Most of the patients were garbed in pajamas or some other nightwear and house shoes. But, I knew better. Once we were in our rooms for bedtime, I kept on my T-shirt and knee-length shorts from earlier. I slipped on a pair of sneakers, and then waited for the sirens to blow.

After twelve months of stay in a psychiatric institution located about ninety miles outside Memphis, Tennessee, I'd had enough. The judge sentenced me to a five-year stint in the psych ward after having killed Nick Murphy, Cole's good friend and co-worker, as well as for organizing the murder of Glenda Patterson, Cole's wife. I was also sentenced to serve another fifteen years in federal prison immediately upon completing treatment in the nuthouse. The judge said my mental illness wasn't severe enough to do all of my time in an asylum, so the remainder would have to be done upstate. But, he was a lie. All I wanted to do was give birth to my baby, which I did, and then spend a few months preparing and planning for my escape, so I could be with my child and the love of my life, Colby Patterson.

Earlier that day, I was given the privilege to assist one of the kitchen workers with lighting the birthday cake that had been ordered for all the patients who had birthdays in that month. The kitchen worker took the lighter from me once I was done, and then placed it into her pocket. I used my pick-pocketing skills to help the lighter mysteriously disappear, but the worker didn't notice it was gone before I had a chance to hide it in my sock. Just before bedtime, I waited outside the staff restroom for one of the aide's to come out. I pretended to be drinking from the water fountain as she stepped out.

"Hurry up, Jolley. It's almost bedtime," she said.

I lifted my head. "Okay. Almost done," I responded, wiping water from my mouth."

She let the restroom door slowly swing closed behind her and walked off. I quickly placed my foot into the door, preventing it from closing and locking. I hurt my big toe in the process, but a little pain ain't never killed nobody. I just hopped right on in and began my dirty work. I dumped the whole stack of paper towels into the trash then lit them on fire. I slid the plastic trashcan so that it would keep the door propped open until it melted or would be discovered. My work there was done, so I carefully sneaked away. I went to another staff restroom and hung out by the water fountain until another aide went inside and came out. I managed to sneak inside and started another fire, placing the can into the doorway there as well.

As I sneaked off this time, I met an aide coming around the corner. This was the one I would've preferred not to run into. She was the mean one—old, pale and wrinkled—probably from frowning all the time. I was used to her bad attitude, and I also knew she might be a little more difficult to fool. I blocked her view of the restroom and stalled her.

"Hey, um . . . Ms. um . . . um—"

"Walters . . . Ms. Walters." She placed her hands on her hips and turned her lip up on one side.

"Oh, yeah. Ms. Walters, um . . . I was thinking, um . . . is it possible I could have clean sheets tonight?"

She lowered her lip then squinted. "What for, Jolley?" She leaned in to my face. "Didn't we just give you clean sheets last night?"

I backed up and covered my nose. She seemed to have caught the hint that she was much too close, and her breath stunk. "Well, yeah, but um . . . well, this is kind of embarrassing, but I um . . . I wet the bed."

Ms. Walters frowned. "You are not a wetter, Jolley."

"I know, but hey . . . things do happen, don't they?"

"I wish I knew what you were really up to, Jolley, but I'm sure I'll find out soon enough."

"C'mon now, Ms. Walters. What have I done to make you not trust me?"

She huffed. "You're sneaky, Jolley, and you know it."

"Ms. Walters . . . now you know you can't really say I've done something to make you not trust me, can you?"

She huffed again. "Naw, but I don't trust none of y'all." She rolled her eyes before turning around. "Follow me, Jolley, and let this be the last time you so-call wet the bed. Why do you think that happened anyway?"

I hurried behind her. "I don't know, ma'am. I guess I might've had a little too much to drink before going to sleep."

Ms. Walters slowed before we made it to the linen closet and looked at me. "How did you get something to drink? We stopped passing out beverages hours before bedtime."

"I know, but I drink from the fountains, ma'am."

She picked up her pace, leaving me a few steps behind, then spoke over her shoulders. "So, is that why I just saw you coming from down the hall?"

"Yes, ma'am."

We stopped at the linen closet. "Okay. Now I see I'm gonna havta make sure the nurses are keeping a closer eye on you. You're not supposed to be at the water fountains so close to bedtime, especially without supervision."

"Please don't tell on me, Ms. Walters. This is my last time sneaking to the fountains. I promise."

She went into the closet and pulled out clean sheets and a blanket. "Alright. But, don't let me catch you down that way anymore at this hour. You hear me?"

"Yes, ma'am. You've got my word." I smirked.

I hurriedly ran toward my room. On the way, I passed the trash room. The door was ajar, so I peeked in. No one was in there. I had a notion to set the sheets and blanket Ms. Walters gave me on fire. I pulled as much trash as I could out into the hallway along with the sheets and blanket. I flicked the lighter onto one of the sheets. It was hard to set a flame. It burned a little, but the fire wouldn't catch on. I was nervous that someone would turn the corner and catch me. I set the lighter on the sheet a little longer. This time, it created smoke, and I burned my hand, trying to force it to blaze. I looked over at the trash bags and paper then realized I was going about it all wrong. Once I set the paper on fire, the rest was history. I ran to my room and closed the door.

Several minutes went by before I heard some smoke detectors beep, and then the fire alarms at every corner began to blare. The once quiet halls suddenly had all sort of noises bouncing in them—screams, slamming doors, sirens, coughing, and then some. I could hear the panicked voices of the aides and other staff as they rushed to the patients' rooms, yelling for us to get out.

I stood at the edge of the woods with the rest of the hospital population overcome with joy. My plan was near complete. All was left for me to do was ease into the forest.

When I looked up and noticed the staff checking the roll, making each patient sit on the grass as they called their name, I panicked. I decided it was now or never. I inched closer to the woods, and once inside, I ran like a track star.

I didn't know I could still run like that. Tree limbs smacked my body and pointy bushes abused my skin as I ducked and jumped through all that was in my way. I kept moving in spite how tired I'd become. I thought surely someone was fast behind me, but I soon realized the only sounds of feet were that of my own. No one was behind me. Absolutely no one! I kept moving quickly though. There was no way of knowing when the staff would notice I was gone.

I ran about five minutes more, and then my knees buckled from under me. My face nearly smashed a pile of dirt and rocks as I fell, but I resisted the contact by placing my hands in front of me. I decided to just lay and catch my breath. In the moments I lay there, breathing like a mad bull, my skin began to itch and burn as mosquitoes and other flying insects tore into my flesh. I slapped at my skin, but there was no way to protect myself. The only thing to do then was to get up and run some more.

As I ran, I heard sirens. I couldn't tell if they were caused by police, fire or ambulance—or maybe, it was the warning sounds of an escaped patient. Surely they'd called my name in the roll and recognized my disappearance by now. The notion made me run just that much harder. Before I knew it, I was out of the woods, but the sight before me caught me by surprise and startled me all in the same.

Cole

1

---

*I*t had been a little more than a week since receiving the letter from Karma's mental institution, which subpoenaed me to take a paternity test. This put a real strain on my new marriage. Audrie felt betrayed, and I can't say I didn't blame her. Everything happened so fast in our lives—including me marrying her, but I hadn't lied to her. Karma told me she had an abortion. That was what she was supposed to do with the money I gave her. I shouldn't have trusted Karma to get rid of the baby. Abortions go against everything I believe in, but I just couldn't see me having to deal with Karma's crazy ass for eighteen years or more. Lord, knows I didn't want to do it.

It was a Friday evening, and the kids were spending the weekend with their grandparents—the Clarks—Glenda's parents. Since learning I had nothing to do with Glenda's murder, the Clarks made efforts to get along with me. Neither of us could truly get past Karma's deadly rage, but we knew Glenda would want us to try to move on with our lives. So, when I found love again with Audrie, I married her. However, the recent revelation of a new baby with Karma began to eat at the core of the love Audrie and I shared.

I had just finished a hot shower, and my stomach roared for the food I smelled floating from the kitchen. "Good evening," I said as I entered and took a seat. Audrie didn't respond. Even as she set my dinner plate before me, she wouldn't even look at me. "Thanks, sweetie," I said just as she set the plate down. Still, she didn't respond. "I said: 'Thanks, sweetie,'" I offered again.

"Mm-hmm," she replied dry-like.

I decided to just eat my dinner in silence as I'd done for the past week. The silence offered room for many thoughts. *Possible paternity?* I didn't want to believe it. I wondered how much more drama could I stand.

"Dinner is good, sweetie," I said in hopes to get some type of response. She just kept her eyes on her plate.

Audrie looked beautiful as she sat, eating her dinner. Her smooth, dark skin was what I called a silk-chocolate color. Just rubbing my hands across her arms or soft shoulders turned me on every time. I watched carefully as she placed each forkful of the mouth-watering lasagna she'd cooked into her mouth. She was gorgeous, but she also looked sad. What hurt me the most was the fact that I couldn't change things. In fact, if I could, I would've gone back in time and made sure to be a better husband to my deceased wife, Glenda. Perhaps if I had paid attention to her concern with all the aggravating phone calls, I would've discovered Karma's deceit long before she had a chance to strike. But, it was all done, and one thing I needed to learn how to do was stop beating myself up.

Audrie jumped from the table, washed her plate then excused herself from the kitchen without saying a word. I ate my dinner in a hurry then marched right behind her. I walked into the bedroom just in time to see her go into the bathroom and close the door. Not long after that, I could hear the shower running. I sat on the edge of the bed, thinking. *Things can't go on like this. I made a mistake by not listening to Glenda. I can't afford more mistakes like that.*

After saying my prayers, I climbed into bed. Audrie walked out of the restroom, wearing one of her big T-shirts and a pair of cotton pajama pants—this was the total opposite of what I'd become accustomed to during our six months of marital bliss. But that all changed the day I received that letter. She slid into bed, barely speaking.

"Goodnight." She offered the same low, solemn tone as she had over the last week.

"Goodnight," I responded.

"Don't forget to turn off the TV before you go to sleep."

I sighed. "Audrie." I stroked her side. "Sit up for a minute. It's time we clear the air . . . once and for all. It's been more than a week, and I can't take living like this anymore."

She eased her body up, but she kept her eyes on the comforter. "I really don't have anything to say, Cole."

"I figured as much. And I'm okay with that. Just listen to me."

"I'm listening." She remained on her side.

"Audrie, it's been over a week now, and you still won't even look at me?"

9

She slowly turned to face me and lifted her eyes. "Cole, I'm hurting."

"I know you are, Audrie, and that's why I think we should talk. I need you to understand that I haven't deceived you. I never wanted a baby with Karma. You know how slick that woman is. I gave her money—I swear I did. I just don't know what happened after that. I can't even remember how to add up the months to see if they match. I'm so confused—more confused than you might be right now."

"But, Cole, a baby with Karma? Think about that for a second. Do you know how rigid our lives will be from this day forward? That girl will give us hell from behind the concrete walls that hold her. Steel and nothing else will be enough to hold her back. Our lives would be in danger."

"Audrie, please. Don't go speaking stuff like that over us. That mental institution is secured. I don't worry about things like that. Besides, she'll be joining the regular prison population after she gets her five years of treatment."

"Hmph. Who knows what kind of mind she'll have then. Institutionalizing her didn't help the first time—after she murdered her parents in that house fire."

"I hear you, Audrie. I'm just saying we don't need to concern ourselves with Karma. It's the child who didn't ask to be here that we need to concentrate on."

"Well, I guess we really don't have a choice, do we? I mean, you've already been subpoenaed, so it's not like this whole situation is going away."

"I believe it will, sweetie."

She twisted her lips. "Cole? How?"

"Audrie, I that baby isn't mine."

"I wish I could believe that, but until that paternity test is done, I'm afraid to get my hopes up."

"I understand. How about we just stay prayerful?"

"You think I'm not? Cole, I should've been the one to have your next child. Not only that, but do you really think I want to be tied to Karma?"

"No, sweetie. I know you wouldn't." We were silent.

"I know you love me, Cole, and I hope you know I love you. Just know that with the way I feel, we'll probably argue about this baby issue a thousand times more."

I stroked her chin. "True. I just want to hear from you that no matter what the results are, you'll still be by my side. I do love you, Audrie, and my love isn't just tied to needing you—I *want* you and only you to be in my world."

There was a long pause before she answered. "I said 'for better or worse,' didn't I?" She gave a half smile. "I'm not going anywhere. I ain't happy though—right now, I'm a long way from it."

"I know, baby, but we're going to get through this. I'll make sure you're happy."

"How?"

"I don't know." I kissed her lips. "But I'll spend a lifetime trying to figure it out. Your happiness is important to me. I need you to know that, okay?" I kissed her lips again.

"Okay," she said softly between my repeated kisses.

I lifted her T-shirt and met an undershirt. "Damn, Audrie, what's all this for? Were you that bent on me not getting any?"

"Yep. I didn't want you to see a nipple or nothing that could possibly turn you on. I'm sorry, but when I'm mad, I don't wanna give you none."

"Audrie, that's not right. You're not supposed to do me like that. Didn't Pastor just preach a sermon about that not long ago?"

"Mm-hmm."

"Oh, you remember, huh? Still doesn't bother you?"

"Well . . . it does, but it's hard turning my feelings off and on like that."

"I tell you what: let's not go to bed without clearing the air anymore. I went through that with Glenda, and I had to learn the hard way that the last thing we say to each other should always be kind. Whatever our issues are, let's agree to talk them out that day. No more hard feelings by bedtime, okay?"

"Okay. I can do that."

"Great. Now take that mess off, and c'mere," I said, removing my pajama bottom.

Audrie giggled. "You miss me, daddy?"

"I don't know. Why don't you climb on top of me and find out?"

She giggled some more as she removed every stitch of cotton that hugged her body, including her socks.

"Now see, that's what I'm talking about. Let me see those pretty toes." Her toes danced with a coat of bright red polish. "Hell yeah . . . that's my baby. C'mere, girl."

Karma

2

---

*J*ust outside of the woods, I saw red, flashing lights coming toward me in a hurry. I dove onto the ground and tried to mesh myself into the tall, uncut grass. I squeezed my eyes shut as I listened to the sirens zoom by. I knew then where I was. When the sirens were a great distance from me, I got up and dusted myself off. I looked around and smiled to myself. It felt good to be standing there—a free woman—standing on the outskirt of Highway 64. *I did it*, I thought as cars and trucks whizzed by me. *I really did it!*

I had a notion to hitch-hike, but then I looked down at myself. *Who would pick me up?* I wondered. *I look a mess—thrown away.* I was dirty and itchy. I couldn't stop scratching the mosquito bites as they swelled all over me. I hadn't thought about wearing sleeves and long pants since I would be running through the woods. I rubbed my skin all over instead of scratching. Scratching would break my skin, and I didn't want Cole to see me with marks on me.

I needed to catch a ride and get off the side of the highway. I wasn't thrilled about riding with a stranger, but I stuck out my thumb anyway. I had no other choice. Almost immediately, an eighteen-wheeler slowed and stopped just a few feet past where I stood. I ran to the truck as quickly as I could. I climbed onto the step then lifted the door latch. A middle-aged, sandy-haired, blue-eyed man stared me in the face.

"Where ya tryna get to, sweet thang?" he asked with a country twang.

"Memphis," I answered, giving him the saccharine tone that always worked with men I encountered.

"Well, hop in. I'm on my way to Memphis. I could use a little company."

I smiled inside as I climbed into the rig and closed the door. He pulled back into traffic, and then introduced himself.

"My name is Daniel, suga. What's yours?"

"Kar—" I started, almost telling on myself. "Kareen Patterson."

"Nice to meet you, Kareen Patterson." He stretched his hand for me to shake it. "I'm Daniel Boone."

I scowled, snatching my hand from him. "Look muthafucka," I screamed. "Don't play with me. Are you one of them psychos who pick up strangers then killed 'em and put 'em out on the side of the road?"

Daniel placed a slow, even-spread smile across his face. "Is that what you think?"

"Pull this shit over! Right now." He kept driving. "Did you hear me? I will cut you from asshole to appetite, if you don't pull this muthafucka over right now!"

Daniel didn't stop. He continued driving, and only moments later, he began to laugh. I glanced at the door and noticed it was locked. I had thoughts of unlocking it, and then jumping out, but given Daniel was driving at about seventy miles per hour, I knew jumping would only be suicide. He must've sensed what I was thinking.

"Listen," he said. "I'm not a serial killer, if that's what you think. I only told you my name is Daniel Boone because I know you gave me a fake name." I looked at him, wondering how he knew. He glanced at me then placed his eyes back on the road. "You look as if you just came up outta them woods back there, lady. You running from somebody or what?" I didn't answer. "I wonder could the psycho be *you*." He laughed some more.

"Just let me out," I answered. "I don't need your help. I'll walk. I want out now!"

"You want out or what? Oh, that's right—you gon' cut me from asshole to appetite." He laughed hysterically for a minute then said, "Well, I might be worried 'cept you ain't got no pockets. Where the knife coming from, sweet thang? Your shoe?"

"I might have one cuffed inside my bra. You don't know."

"Listen. Relax. I don't care if you just broke outta the nuthouse." My eyes bucked. He turned and looked at me. "I thank you a pretty li'l thang—too pretty to be all that crazy. I can't imagine what you did to get yourself locked up in that place."

"I didn't do anything, and I ain't crazy," I snapped.

"Is that right? Well, it don't matter much to me none if you wanna check out early. In fact, I'm glad you did. I've come a thousand miles by myself, and now I got company as I do this last leg into Memphis."

I sat silently for a minute. The many mosquito bites I incurred aggravated me some more. I scratched my legs a little and rubbed my arms. Daniel noticed.

"You a'ight? Looks like you got yourself some kind of itch there."

"It's just mosquito bites. I got 'em coming through those woods, so don't worry. I ain't got nothing you can catch." I was silent for a few seconds and then, it dawned on me that he had to want something. "What I owe you anyway?"

"Huh?"

"You want something. I know you do, so just gon' tell me now. What you want from me for this ride?"

He chuckled a bit. "I wouldn't ask ya to do anything you wouldn't want to do."

"That's not what I asked you. What do you want?"

"Ever peeled back the head of a white dick before?" He smiled, and I almost threw up.

I thought about how pink and musty his flesh must be, given how long he'd been driving, and then I gagged for real. "Naw. I don't even know how to give head," I lied.

"Aw, I can't believe that. You a young thang, but I still can't believe you all that innocent."

"Well, I am."

"You a virgin, too?"

I wanted to lie and say yes, but I didn't know if he'd put me out on the side of the road, and I figured I might need another favor from him besides the ride. I went ahead and told the truth. "I've done it before."

"You any good?" he asked, grinning.

"Maybe."

He hissed as he glanced at me. "You got pretty lips, too. Sho wouldn't mind 'em wrapped around this thang here," he said, squeezing his crotch.

"Look. You said you wouldn't ask me to do anything I wouldn't want to do. Besides, you ain't even washed that thang. I ain't puttin' my mouth on it."

"If I stop at a restroom and washed it, would you do it—"

"No! Un-un. I'll screw you—with a rubber, but don't ask me to do anything else."

Daniel smiled. "A'ight, sweet thang. I'll take what I can get. Mind if I pull over now?"

"Hell yeah I mind. Get me to Memphis first, and then I'll take care of you."

"A'ight, suga. I ain't got no problem with that. Just thought I'd ask."

We rode in silence for nearly an hour, and then it dawned on me that I needed a change of clothes. I wondered what it would take to convince Daniel to stop at a Wal-mart or some other twenty-four-hour store and buy me an outfit. As I pondered my approach on the subject, Daniel got a call on his CB radio.

"Hambone calling Great Dane. Come in, Great Dane."

Daniel picked up his mic and responded. "This is Great Dane. Go 'head, Hambone."

"Man, you get caught up in traffic on I-64? I'm stuck behind a roadblock."

"A roadblock?" Daniel questioned.

"Yeah. I done asked what this search is all about. The cops telling me something 'bout a fire at the mental hospital just over the way . . . say a patient done escaped, too."

"What?" Daniel responded then looked at me. "Naw, I ain't 'round those parts. I done got clear of that mess. Guess I'll see you whenever you can make it in, good buddy. I'll wait on ya at the truck stop on I-78."

"That's a 10-4, pal. I'll hit you back when I get closer to Memphis."

"10-4. Over." Daniel placed the mic back into its receiver. He looked at me again. "Seems you got everythang all jammed up back a ways, sweet thang. You ain't have nothing to do with starting that fire, did ya?"

"Now how would I start a fire in that huge place?"

"I don't know. I ain't ever been locked up in a crazy house. I'm just askin' ya."

"Listen. I need to talk about something else."

"What is it?"

"I need a change of clothes. You think you can help me?"

"You mean buy you something else to wear?"

"Yeah—I mean, I know you ain't got nothing back there in that sleeper I can wear, do you?"

"Naw. I don't make it a habit of keeping women's clothes in my rig. It's pretty late. How you expect to get something?"

"I was thinking you could go in a Wal-mart and pick me something."

"Me—pick you something? Now hold on—"

"Come on, Daniel. I mean, your name *is* Daniel, isn't it?"

"Yeah. That's my first name."

"Daniel, you want me to get caught? You heard your friend say there're reports of my escape. C'mon now. Don't get me caught before I can break you off some of this," I said, rubbing between my legs.

Daniel smiled. "A'ight. I guess since you put it that way. But, you gon' havta tell me yo' size and everythang, and don't be mad if I come outta there with the wrong stuff. I don't know how to pick clothes for women."

"Cool. I'm sure you'll do fine."

About an hour later, Daniel was out of the store with my change of clothes, and we were pulling into the truck stop he'd mentioned to his pal on the CB. The place was well-lit and hoarded with big trucks. Daniel managed to find a parking spot, and then he began taking off his shoes. I was turned off even more. He caught me frowning.

"Aw, sweet thang, don't worry. My feet don't stank. I make sure of it. See," he said as he plucked one boot off. "Smell anythang?" He smiled, shaking his head. "Ya don't, do ya?"

"Naw. Thank goodness," I answered, scratching my arms.

"What's da matter? Aw, I shoulda gotcha something for that itch, huh? I can go into the store over there and see if they got—"

"No . . . no . . . I don't need anything. Let's just get this over with. You got condoms?"

"Of course, I got —"

"Well, come on. Hurry up."

I took off my clothes and kept my gym shoes where I could easily get to them.

"Whatcha doing with them thangs?" Daniel pointed to my shoes.

"Oh, I was just getting them out of our way," I lied.

Truth: I had a plan in the making.

Cole

3

I watched her. I knew she could feel my glare as I lurked about her store. I crept freely, having no fear she'd seen me walk into the candy shop then head straight to the back. I ducked just as she turned around. I eyed her some more. A tall drink of water is what she was—no, better yet—a tall glass of chocolate milk. She kept her routine as best as she could, counting down her drawer for the night. *Has she seen me yet?* I wondered. *Maybe I should make a little noise to alert her now.* Before I could make another move, she spotted me, kneeling behind a chair.

"Sir," she called, standing on her tiptoes to peek at me. "It's closing time. Is there something I can help you with?"

I slouched at the base of the rack, not moving a muscle. I didn't answer. She had no idea what I was up to, and more importantly, I planned to do whatever it took to make sure she'd go along with my little scheme.

She called to me once more, but again I failed to answer. She headed toward the telephone then called to me again. "Sir, I'm closing the store. Is there something I can help you with?"

I rose and began walking toward her in a slow, deliberate pace. Only the sound of my breathing could be heard, making the situation seem even more eerie. She picked up the phone and placed her finger on a button.

I stepped closer. She was frozen solid. She looked at the phone then back at me—her stalker—as I approached. I finally spoke. "Excuse me, ma'am," I said in a soothingly deep voice. "I hate to disturb you, but before you place that call, will you assist me in the back?"

I noticed she swallowed hard. Then she responded, "What can I do for you, sir?"

"Well, I was just looking at the Jelly Bellies, but I didn't see a particular flavor I like."

"And what flavor is that?"

"Dark chocolate."

"Excuse me?"

"You heard me." I eyed her from head to toe. "In fact, make that silk chocolate."

She gave me a knowing look then glanced at her arms. "Excuse me, sir, but are you referring to me?"

I nodded slowly. She lifted the phone then pressed a number. Her finger started for a second number, but my next words stopped her cold. "I wouldn't do that if I were you." My calm never left.

"W-w-whhyy?" I found it cute that she could hardly form words to speak.

"Do you really think calling the police will stop me from doing what I came to do to you?"

"What did you come to do?"

I flashed a wide smile before answering. "I'm here to fulfill your wildest dream—you know—to have un-tamed, passionate sex with a good-looking, complete stranger in the back of your store.

Her mouth flew open, and she hung up the phone simultaneously. "How . . . how . . . where did you—"

"How I found out is not important. What matters most is that I'm here, and I'm willing." I stared into her anxious eyes as she heaved. "Relax," I said, easing her hand into mine. "My name is Tony. I won't hurt you. I aim to please."

I pulled her close, sticking my tongue in her mouth. My lips met no resistance as she kissed me back. Weeks had passed since my last sexual encounter, and my body wanted to melt into hers. I yearned her heated flesh. I imagined her insides throbbing for me.

"I don't know if I should do this," she said after breaking our kiss a full two minutes later.

"Why not? You want me. You know you want me." I kissed her some more.

At that point, she took the lead. "In my office."

I stepped behind her to the area she called her office. She reached under her black skirt and removed her panties. After dropping my slacks and underwear, I stood with an erection so strong, she looked scared. She even gasped. Her eyes repeatedly took toward my midsection.

"What's that?" she asked.

"It's called a build-up, sweetie," I answered. "This is what happens when a man is made to wait a long time. What about you?"

"It's been weeks," she said in a sheepish tone.

"Same here." I inched over to her with my pants wrapped around my ankles. I unfastened her white button-down then relieved her breasts of her bra. "Beautiful," I whispered as I studied them with my hands. "Simply beautiful."

She became weak, grabbing any and everything she could for support. I pulled her skirt above her waist. "Damn, baby, you're sexy as hell. Where've you been all my life?"

She trembled with heat. She wanted me—I could tell. But I wasn't done teasing her.

"You're hot," I said. "But I'm not going to give it to you yet. I've come a long way just to have my way with you. I'm gonna take things slow. I'll please you all night if I have to." I looked around the room for somewhere to lay her. "Is this your desk?"

She smiled, and then giggled. "Yeah."

"Cool. Get up there and bend over."

She did as told, and I could tell she was bracing herself for what was about to happen next.

"Oh, I can't believe this is about to go down. Am I dreaming? Please tell me . . . is this a dream?"

She got the answer just a few minutes later when I released my ankles from my pants, and then hopped on top of the desk with her. I entered her with long, hard strokes. I gave her all of me, making sure she understood this was no dream. The intense passion had barely begun, but already she was pleading for it to last an eternity.

"Aaaaahhhh, yeeeeessss, pleeeease, don't stop. Harder . . . I need it harder. Don't stop." This ride was wild. She held on for dear life.

Though her face was pruned, I knew her body was on cloud nine, praying to make it toward ten. In fact, I had the mind to take her on to heaven—I was sure she wouldn't mind.

Her moans took me to another level. I was going crazy. "No, no, no . . . not yet," I moaned. "Too soon . . . it's too soon to—no! One hundred, ninety-nine, ninety-eight—"

I began counting backward from one hundred, trying to make my mind go elsewhere. It didn't help. We collapsed together, but I panicked as I tried to catch my breath.

"I'm sorry," I said, panting. "I'm . . . sorry, sweetie. I know your fantasy was short-lived. Just . . . just . . . give me . . . a minute. I'll make it . . . up to you."

"Cole, get up," Audrie screamed. "Just get up."

"My bad, sweetie," I said, rolling off her. "You shouldn't have made me wait so long. You still got yours, didn't you?"

"Yeah, but I still wasn't ready for it to end."

"Dang, girl. That was climax number two, wasn't it? I know it was for me."

"So, why are you counting?" she said with an attitude.

"Look. I said we can start again. Just give me a minute." My breathing slowed a bit. "How long did you have the candy shop worker fantasy anyway?"

Her attitude quickly changed into laughter. "I don't know. I just thought of it one day. Thanks for putting on that shirt and slacks. You were so fine, *Tony*."

"Not as fine as you, my dear, with the black skirt and white blouse uniform." I had to laugh myself.

"Cole," she said.

"Huh?"

"Chocolate Jelly Bellies? You couldn't think of anything else?"

"Uh, no, I couldn't, but I saw your amusement when I suggested the bed was your desk."

We both had a hardy laugh — until something caught Audrie's attention on television.

"Cole, turn that up!" she screamed, pointing at our thirty-two-inch flat screen. "That's Karma! Turn it up!"

I hurriedly grabbed the remote on the nightstand near my side of the bed then pressed the volume button.

"Again folks," the reporter said, "a fire has broken out at the West Tennessee Mental Institution just ninety miles outside of Memphis, and it is believed that one patient, Karma Jolley, has either escaped or is missing in the building. Stay tuned for further details at ten on this breaking news story."

The television returned to its regularly scheduled program, but Audrie and I sat, staring as if the reporter was still there. Now it was my turn to wonder if I was dreaming. One thing was for sure: Audrie and I were in for a long night because neither of us would get any sleep.

Karma

4

*A*s Daniel lay in the back of his rig, I straddled him and commenced to riding him into the middle of next week. He wheezed and hemmed and hawed and heaved—all in all, his breathing scared me.

"Damn, girl," he yelled. I pumped him again. "Damn, girl," he repeated.

He yelled and screamed some more. I thought he was having a heart attack, but every time I tried to stop, he begged me not to. Three minutes—that's all it took to get him off. I know because I watched each minute pass on the digital watch he took off his arm and placed beside us on the bed.

Once we were done, I jumped off him, making sure the condom was still in tact. The last thing I needed was to get pregnant by a country white man I didn't know. My mission was far different than that. I had a man and a family already, and it was time to reclaim them.

Daniel seemed to be knocked out cold. I needed to be sure though. I placed my hand just above his nose to see if he'd sense me. I felt his hot breath on the palm of my hand, but he didn't move. I called him.

"Daniel," I said in a medium tone. He didn't budge. "Daniel," I called again, just a bit louder. He still didn't move, and he began to snore.

I eased off the bed then reached for my bra and panties. After putting them on, I reached into the plastic bag, which contained the clothes Daniel bought me and pulled out a black T-shirt and black legging-type pants—nothing of my taste, but it would have to do. I pulled the T-shirt over my head and realized it was slightly too big, so I gathered it in the back then made a knot, exposing my belly button. The bought the pants in size small, so they fit just fine. After putting on my gym shoes, I looked over to Daniel. He was out like a light.

I eased to the front of the rig then opened the glove compartment. Just like I figured, Daniel's wallet lay inside. I opened it and discovered six-hundred dollars in large bills. I placed the money into my bra, and then put the wallet back just before carefully closing the compartment.

I inched to the back of the cab to spy on Daniel once more. He hadn't moved from the bed with the exception of one of his legs hanging off. I knew I needed to make my move and make it fast. I left the truck in a hurry, barely closing the door for fear shutting it would wake Daniel.

I hopped off the step of the rig. It was dark and warm outside. All life seemed to have stopped. Big rigs lined the parking lot as far as I could see. I had a notion to peruse some of the other cabs for money. Since it was pretty late, I knew in all likelihood the drivers were asleep. I walked the lot, choosing my targets carefully. If the trucks were running and the inside lights were on, they were off my radar. I spotted a few trucks in the back lot, out of view of the front of the store. The lights were off, but I could hear them running. I knew in all likelihood the drivers were asleep and burning the air conditioners.

I was right. I could hear the driver of the first rig snoring before I could get the door opened all the way. The door was conveniently unlocked. I was careful not to make noise as I searched the rig for valuables and money. There were no valuables that I could see, but the money part was easy. I found one thousand dollars hidden in an envelope placed under the driver's seat. *Too easy,* I thought as I smiled. I left that truck, barely closing the door, and headed for the second truck.

As I opened the door to the second rig, I wondered if any of the drivers ever locked their doors. At this point, I was extremely glad I made the decision to hit them up. This driver's CB radio was on, and I heard noises coming from the back of the rig. I sat still, listening, and the noises soon became apparent. This driver had a prostitute in the back with him, and they were having sex.

"That's it, daddy," I heard her say. "Work it . . . work it."

"You like that, dontcha, girl?" the masculine voice said.

"Yeah, daddy. You doing me good."

"Un-huh. I knew it. You can't get enough of this, can you?"

"Naw, daddy. I can't get enough. Give me all of this good thang."

I couldn't see her, but whoever she was, she sure sounded like she knew how to act. Given the radio had multiple conversations going on, I didn't fear being heard upfront. I did what I had to do. His compartment made a slight noise as I opened it, so I was afraid to try to shut it. There was nothing in it, and there was nothing under the seats. I spotted the driver's pants on the floor. I checked his pants for a wallet and lucked up. His wallet had four hundred dollars. I placed it into the other side of my bra.

Just as I secured the money and collected my envelope of money stolen from the previous rig, I heard Daniel's voice over the CB radio.

"Breaker, breaker, one-nine!" he yelled.

The guy from the back hushed the woman. "Sssh. Somebody sound like they in trouble."

"I didn't hear nothing," she said.

"Well, I did."

"Breaker, breaker, one-nine!" Daniel yelled again.

The guy was louder. "See! I told ya. Now be quiet."

Daniel sounded panicked. "This is Great Dane, sittin' at the Stop N Go rest stop on Highway 78. I just been robbed. I repeat. If you hounds are at the Stop N Go rest stop on I-78, lock your cabs now . . . I've been bitten by a lot lizard!"

I wanted to break and run, but I didn't want to alert the driver and prostitute of my presence. I heard him fussing at her.

"A lot lizard? Getcho' ass up! Is it you?" he asked.

"Naw, daddy. You heard him say it just happened. I been in here with you for the past hour."

"I don't know. Move. Let me ask Dane something."

Just then, the curtain snatched open. The driver and I locked eyes. We were both frozen for a second, and then my mind told me now was the time to run.

"Hey!" he screamed after me, grabbing my arm. "Hey . . . hold it!"

He only had one hand clamped at my wrist, but his grip was unbreakable. I squirmed and punched at his hand, but it was no use. This man was much too strong for me. He picked up the CB mic with the other hand and called to Daniel.

"Punisher to Great Dane! I got a hold of that lizard. I'm in the back of the lot. Hurry up. This one is aiming to get away."

"On my way, Pun." Daniel sounded as if he was spitting flames.

I knew I had to get away by any means necessary. I swung at this guy with everything I had, landing punches in his face and neck, but he wasn't fazed. So, I sunk my teeth into his hand. He screamed like a bitch, pulling up on my head. I didn't let him go until I drew blood. I spit on him then jumped out of the truck, but only to face more trouble. I looked up and spotted a small army of guys, including Daniel running my way.

I switched into track star mode, darting around the store and then across six lanes of traffic on I-78. Those guys were just as daring as I was because the oncoming cars didn't stop them from coming behind me. It did slow them

31

down a bit though. Once across the road, I ran down a steep hill that led to a damn. I went under the overpass and prepared to duck into the muddy water. I waited until the voices and trampling feet got closer, and then I took a deep breath and held my nose just before going under.

I could hear muffled voices. "Do you see her?" one of them asked.

"Naw. I can't see a damned thing," another one said.

"Maybe she went into the woods yonder," someone else said.

"Aw, hell, I ain't going in there this time of night."

I could only hope they would give up the search quickly, so I could come up for air. I waited until I just couldn't take it anymore before popping up. I could see the men heading back up the hill. I took a few deep breaths then went back under just in case one of them decided to look back. By the time I thought they were gone, I climbed out of the water and hid on the pavement just under the overpass. It was dark as hell, but I wasn't coming from under there until I was certain the coast was clear.

My money was wet. I separated the bills, and then scrambled rocks to place on top of each of them so they wouldn't blow away as they dried. I had more than enough money I could work with. The next thing was to come up with another look and identity, so I could go find my man.

Cole

5

---

*T*he news of Karma's breakout was stunning, to say the least. Audrie and I both had early mornings, so we needed our sleep. Sleep didn't happen. Audrie tossed and turned all night. And when she managed to dose, she'd jump up only minutes later, screaming from a nightmare. I promised her I'd stay awake to listen for possible strange noises, but even that didn't make Audrie comfortable. Bottom line—we were going to have to leave that house.

I rolled over and noticed it was four A.M. Audrie was just chatting with me, but then I heard mild snoring. I was confident Karma didn't know where we lived. Surely, the hospital hadn't told her our new address, I thought. I decided it would be okay to get some sleep. I put my arm over Audrie's waist then closed my eyes.

RING. RING. RING.

It was the phone. Audrie and I were so startled, we both jumped out of the bed at the same time.

"What? What's going on?" she asked.

"Nothing, sweetie. It's the phone. It's just the phone. I'll get it."

I walked over to the nightstand then reached for the cordless phone without checking the caller ID. "Hello, I answered." Audrie stood, watching, holding her chest.

"Colby, it's Mrs. Clark."

"Mrs. Clark?"

"Yes. Sorry to bother you this time of morning, but Shawna has a slight fever. I've been monitoring her all night, and it's a little higher than it was before she went to bed."

I sat on the edge of the bed. "Have you taken her temperature?"

"Yes, and the thermometer says 101.5."

"Okay, I might need to come get her and take her to the minor emergency room."

"Well, she's asleep, Colby. I was just wondering if she can take some of this Children's Motrin I have here. I have some left over from when I kept my great-niece, but I wasn't sure if Shawna could take it. I know you usually give her Children's Tylenol."

"Yes, ma'am. She can have the Motrin. That would be fine. Did she get into your pool at all yesterday?"

"Yes, and I was hoping I wouldn't have to tell you because she wanted to get in it so bad. I knew that water wouldn't be good for her ears. I felt so sorry for her watching the other kids in the pool though."

"Mrs. Clark, her ears may be infected now. Go ahead and give her the Motrin, and I'll pick her up in a few hours to see if I can get her seen."

"Well, alright. Call me when you are on your way, so I can have her ready."

"Yes, ma'am."

When we hung up, Audrie couldn't wait to question me. She stood on the other side of the bed.

"What? What's wrong?" she asked, her face filled with worry.

"Lay down, sweetie. That was Mrs. Clark. She just wanted to know if she could give Shawna some medicine for her fever."

Audrie let out an exasperated sigh. "I can't live like this, baby. I know it's not your fault, but I can't spend my nights with one eye open and one eye closed." She plopped onto the bed.

"I know, sweetheart. I just don't know what we need to do."

"I do. We've got to leave this house! I mean, it might take her some time to find us, now that we're in a new neighborhood, but last I remember, that girl can find a way to get what she wants."

"Audrie, I've already thought of all of that, but don't you think if Karma is watching us, she'll follow us to a hotel or wherever?"

"Well, maybe we should just leave town for the weekend."

"And go where?"

"I don't know. It doesn't matter. I just want to get away from here."

"Sweetie, you do know that when we come back, we'll have the same problem, right?"

"Maybe. Maybe not. I know Karma is being hunted down like a runaway slave right now. Surely, she'll be caught before the weekend is out, and then it will be okay to return home."

I sighed. "If that will make you feel better, sweetie, we can certainly do that. Let's just make sure Shawna is okay, and we'll go from there."

Audrie quickly sat up and looked toward the hallway. "Did you hear that?"

"Hear what? Did you—"

"Ssshhh!" She held her finger to her lips then whispered. "Listen."

I remained silent, hoping Audrie was only hearing things. After a few seconds, the atmosphere was still. I didn't hear a thing. I couldn't just sit there though. I had a notion to run into my son's room for his baseball bat. Audrie was swift behind me. I closed my son's closet door then turned around with the bat in my hand. Audrie was so close, she startled me.

"Damn, Audrie." I took a few seconds to catch my breath. "Sweetie, please go back into the bedroom while I check things out."

"Cole, I heard a car pull into our driveway while we were on our way in here," she whispered.

"What? It can't be. It's not even four-thirty in the morning."

"Baby, I'm telling you: Someone's out there."

I headed to peek out of Gavin's bedroom window, but it was no use. I knew I couldn't see the driveway from his window, but I didn't know what else to do. I eased into the hallway and headed toward the living room. Bright headlights shined through the front window, but someone shut them off just before I made it to the entryway.

Audrie was too close on me. She stepped on my heels each time I made a step. "Sweetie, please. I need for you to go back into the bedroom."

"Baby, I'm scared, and I don't want to leave you," she whispered. She had tears in her eyes.

"Okay, but you're too close. I don't want to hurt you if I have to swing this bat."

Audrie took a few steps back then stood in place. I walked over to the window then eased back the curtains just enough so the visitor couldn't see me. I knew I had just spoken to Mrs. Clark. She couldn't have made it over to my home so quickly. Plus, we hadn't discussed her bringing Shawna home.

I didn't recognize the car that was parked halfway up my driveway. It appeared to be black, and no one was inside. I turned to look at Audrie. She mouthed, "Who is it?" But she didn't release a sound. I shrugged.

"There's a car out there, but no one is inside," I whispered.

Just as I turned to peek through the curtains again, BOOM. A thunderous bang hit my front door. Audrie let out a deafening scream, and I jumped back, releasing the curtains and leaping from the window.

"Sweetie, grab the phone," I yelled. "Get the phone now. We may need the police."

Audrie seemed to run around in circles for a few seconds then she made it over to the stand with the cordless phone. I went over to the front door, determined to find out what made that noise. I could hear Audrie's breathing all the way across the room. She might've heard mine, too. I was just as afraid because all I had was a bat—absolutely no match for a gun, if the intruder had one.

I thought about what Audrie said earlier. *"Steel and nothing else will be enough to hold her back. Our lives would be in danger."* I began to fear Audrie was right. Although crime happen everywhere, we lived in a great neighborhood, and the only person I could think of that could finagle past the guard at the community gate and target our house at that time of the morning had to be Karma. I turned off the alarm then unlocked the door.

"Baby, what are you doing?" Audrie said, crying from the hall entrance. "Let me call the police to check it out."

"Hold on, sweetie. I'm not going far. I just want to see if I can tell what happened."

"Noooooo! Baby, pleeeeaaaseee," Audrie screamed.

My mind wouldn't let me rest until I knew what made that noise. I opened my door with a tight grip on the bat. Before I could step out, I heard the car in the driveway backing out. I stepped onto the porch then the driver turned on the headlights, blinding my view. I held my hand over my brows and squinted, trying to see if I could determine who had been at my door. The car stopped, and my heart pounded. I saw the driver's door open.

"Sorry about that, Mr. Patterson," a male voice yelled toward me. "I didn't mean to throw your paper so hard. I was trying to make sure it reached the doorstep."

"Desmond, is that you?" I asked, squinting, still trying to make out the man's face.

"Yes, sir, it is," he answered, then reached into his car and turned off his headlights.

I could see him clearly. "Oh, wow. You're out delivering the morning papers pretty early, aren't you?"

"Yes, sir. My route has changed a little, so I'm in your area first."

"Well, alright." I kneeled to collect the paper.

"I won't be so careless when I toss the paper in the morning, Mr. Patterson."

"Alright. I'm going in before we wake up the rest of the neighbors. Be careful, Desmond."

"Thank you, sir."

He got back into his car, turned on his headlights, and continued to back out of my driveway. I went back into the house and locked the door. As I reset the alarm, Audrie walked over, wiping tears.

"It's alright, sweetie." I helped wipe her tears. "You heard me talking to Desmond, right? That's all it was—his arm was a little too strong when he tossed the paper."

"Cole, this is hard. I can't do this. I refuse to live scared every day."

I wrapped my arms around her. "I know, sweetie. I know."

Damn, I thought. *Haven't I gone through enough for not being all that Glenda needed me to be?* I had no doubt I was a better husband now that I had Audrie, but the past just seemed to keep haunting me—and her name was Karma.

Karma

6

She sort of looked like me, but of course, I was better looking. But she would have to do. I saw her shortly after making it up Highway 78, which turned into Lamar Ave. The black ensemble Daniel bought me came in handy because as I walked up the highway just before dawn, nobody seemed to pay me any attention. It was like I was invisible in the night. Once I made it to a fairly busy gas station, I decided to stop and get something to eat. I had no idea where I was headed. I just needed to be as far away from Daniel and that Stop N Go as possible.

I sat on the curb outside the station, eating a sausage and egg biscuit and orange juice. The clock in the station said it was a quarter till ten once I came out of the restroom. My hair was wild before I purchased a comb and combed it down. As I sat on the curb, contemplating my next move, nobody seemed interested in me still. That was great. I felt no urgency to get up from there.

Then, I saw her pull up to a pump. She walked inside then returned to her car and began filling her tank. She drove a silver-colored Nissan Maximum. Before she could finish pumping her gas, a taxi dropped an attendant at the station for work. I flagged the taxi driver for a ride.

"Where to?" he asked just after I hopped in.

"Wherever that lady is going," I said, pointing at the woman who was pumping gas.

"Ma'am, that's not telling me anything," he said, turning to face me in the backseat.

I went into the damp envelope and peel out a hundred dollar bill. "Listen, Nappy Locks. I don't know where she's going, but I can't lose her, so take this Benjamin and follow her like I asked."

The man brushed his hand over his dreads then took the one hundred dollar bill. He turned and pulled behind the woman without saying another word.

I kept my eyes on her car. She turned up Knight Arnold Road then drove for a while. I could see Perkins Avenue just ahead, but she made a right into the parking lot of the Parkway Village Library. The taxi driver slowed behind her as she turned.

"What now?" he asked.

She pulled into a parking space. "Pull over," I demanded, keeping my eyes on the woman. I watched her walk inside the library. "Hey, can you circle for about ten minutes then pick me back up?"

"I don't know. If somebody calls, I'll have to leave."

"What if I guarantee you another fifty when I come back?"

"I—I—ma'am—"

"Will you do it or not?" I snapped.

"What are you going to do? Are you stalking that lady or something?"

"No. Do I look like a stalker to you?" I thought about my grungy appearance for a second then quickly said, "Don't answer that question. Just let me know if you'll do it."

"Look, I—"

"Hey, if you're not going to do it, I just need to know so I can call for another ride. Perhaps one of your buddies wants to make the money, if you don't. Now, this is my last time asking. Will you do it?"

"Yeah. Go ahead. I'll be here. But, ten minutes, and then I'm gone."

"Cool. I'll be right back."

I got out of the cab, checking my bra for the money I stashed there and patting my front panty line to make sure I could still feel the envelope of money I put there earlier. I released the shirt so that it hung over my stomach, hiding my package.

The library was fairly empty once I got inside. I saw a few people who looked as if they worked there, wandering the aisles, but I hadn't seen the woman I was looking for. *Where'd she go that fast?* I thought. She seemed to have disappeared into thin air. I combed the aisles between the shelves as quickly as I could, but I couldn't find her. I rushed toward the front door to see if she somehow had gotten by me and was back out at her car, but I stopped in my tracks when I noticed her exiting the restroom.

I ducked onto an aisle then pulled a book off the shelf to spy on her. She entered an aisle, seemingly looking for a book. I could only hope this lady didn't spend too much time on the aisle because I needed a way to get close to her before my ten minutes was up.

Finally, she made her way over to a table with a book in her hand. I let her sit there for a couple of minutes, thumbing through the book, and then I sat at the table with her. She looked up at me.

"Hi," she said just before dropping her head back into the book.

"Hi," I responded.

I think I made her uneasy. She shifted in her seat a little, and I could tell she was no longer reading the book. Her eyes were fixed on the pages, but every time I made a new move, like flipping a page in my book, she glanced up at me.

Time was running out. I had to make a move. "Oh, wow, is that Catcher in the Rye by J. D. Salinger?" I asked, complimenting her book choice.

She looked at me. "Yes," she answered.

"I thought so. I love that book. My uncle suggested that I read it some years back, and so I did. I wouldn't mind reading it again."

"Really," she said. "Well, if it's that good, I might as well go ahead and take it home." She stood.

Now was the time to make my move. I jumped up. "I think I'll go see if there is another one on the shelf."

I walked over to the shelves while the woman walked to the check out counter. I watched her hand over her library card and make small talk with the lady at the counter. Once everything was done, I quickly made my way to the counter and pretended I wanted to check out the book in my hand.

Before the lady could get her purse off the counter, I quickly knocked it to the floor, making it seem as if it was an accident. Just like I hoped, all of its contents spilled onto the floor.

"Oh, my goodness," I said, bending to help collect her things. "I'm so sorry."

She didn't seem bothered. I acted quicker than she did gathering her things. She seemed more interested in collecting the many pieces of her Mac Makeup than she did about making sure she had her checkbook. Once we stood, she gave the floor a once-over, seemingly making sure everything had been picked up.

"I'm so sorry, ma'am. I didn't mean to be such a klutz."

"Oh, don't worry about it. This ol' purse has seen worse days in the rain and mud." She laughed. "You have a nice day," she said, turning to leave the library.

The woman at the counter had her back to me as she straightened things on a table against the wall. She turned just as I set the book on the counter.

"Oh, are you two finished already?" she asked. "I thought you were still busy."

"No, ma'am, we're done. Only a few items fell out," I lied. "But, you know what? I don't think I'm going to check out this book. I'll just wait."

She picked up the book. "Are you sure? You know we don't have many copies of *Charlotte's Web* in our library system any more."

I did a double-take and looked at the book in the woman's hand. *What the hell?* I thought. I had no idea what book I picked off the shelf. I collected myself then smiled.

"Yes, I know. It's just that my little girl has too many books to play catch up on already. I've bought her a bunch of books in the past month."

"I see. Well, if you change your mind, just c'mon back."

"I will," I answered.

I walked out, hoping my victim was long gone and hadn't looked in her purse yet. Once outside, I noticed her car was gone, and my cab was pulling up. I hopped in then told the driver to take me to an extended stay on another side of town.

"Another side like where? North Memphis?"

I never lived in North Memphis, but I'd been in the area before. Just like everywhere, North Memphis had its good and rough parts, but I didn't want to be out that way.

"No, I don't think so," I told him.

"What about Whitehaven?"

I was very familiar with Whitehaven. As a matter of fact, I knew everything there was to know about the area after having dealt with Cole. I smiled inside, thinking of my past days with him. I dazed out the window, drifting into deep thought. The driver had to call for my attention.

"Ma'am!"

"Huh?" I was startled.

"You wanna go to Whitehaven or not?" He seemed irritated.

"Yeah. Sure. That will be fine."

I reached into the back of my pants and pulled out the woman's black checkbook holder. Inside were checks, credit cards, and all of her ID, including her driver's license and social security card. *Yes! Chi-ching!* I took a look at her ID picture. She wore a long, dark, Cher-like hair weave, with Chinese-cut bangs. She was twenty-five years old—she only had me by a couple of years—close enough. I read her name. *Robin Tyler. I can rock that,* I thought. Then, it's Robin Tyler, I am.

"Um, excuse me, driver. I need to make a couple of more stops first."

"Where to, ma'am?"

"To the beauty supply store, and then First Tennessee Bank."

"I'll stop off at those places when we get to White-haven."

"Oh, good. Take me to the Golden Beauty Supply on Elvis Presley Boulevard, and there should be a First Tennessee Bank just up the street."

"I'm familiar with both of those."

"Good."

I dazed out the window again. If I was going to be "Robin Tyler," I needed some hair first, and then I was on my way to make a cash withdrawal before the real Robin Tyler put a halt to my access. Hmph. I couldn't wait to assume my new identity. I knew once Cole got one look at me in my new hair and slightly thicker body after having his baby, he wouldn't be able to resist me.

Cole

7

Shawna was fine. Her fever was gone, but I decided she still needed to see a doctor. The last thing I wanted to happen was to get a call from the Clarks about Shawna needing medical attention while Audrie and I were out of town. The doctor at the minor emergency room said her ears showed signs of a premature infection, so he prescribed her some Amoxicillin in liquid form. Shawna was used to the routine, given she'd suffered with her ears a few times before, but she absolutely hated taking the medicine. Mrs. Clark assured me Shawna would be fine while Audrie and I go away.

I didn't tell the Clarks the reason Audrie and I were going away on short notice. I felt that news would only alarm them. I just couldn't give them something else to worry about, but Mr. Clark walked me to my car after I took Shawna back over to their house from her doctor's visit. He wanted to talk to me alone. Audrie was home researching places we could go to, but I had time to chat.

"Colby," he said just as we stopped at the driver's side of my car. "Thelma doesn't know this, but I saw the report about Karma's escape." I dropped my head and shook it. "I'm so glad you didn't mention it when we were in the house."

"No. I wasn't going to do that. I was actually hoping you didn't see the news."

"Well, it's been the talk of the day, but I've kept Thelma away from the news."

"What about her friends and other family? Won't someone call and tell her?"

"I've asked most of them not to tell her. Thelma is still fragile. The thought of Karma being back on the streets would break her heart. She and I both wanted that woman put away for good."

"Me, too, Mr. Clark. She upset my whole world. I'm struggling with bitterness. Glenda . . . Glenda—" I had to pause and collect myself. I became very emotional. "She was my love. My life. She—" I paused again, this time dropping my head to conceal my watering eyes. "She didn't deserve to die."

Mr. Clark patted my shoulder. "I think we're all struggling, Colby."

I took a deep breath and swallowed hard. I had to hold it together because I didn't want Mrs. Clark to peek out the window and see me emotional. I looked at Mr. Clark. His eyes were glassy, too.

"She'll be caught. They can't let a woman like Karma stay on the streets for long."

"Right. I'm holding strong to that belief. I can only imagine how Audrie must feel."

"Mr. Clark, she's devastated. She's nervous and very paranoid."

"Then, this trip should do her some good. You're doing right, Colby. Take your wife away from the stress. Don't worry about the children. You know they're in good hands."

"Yes, sir, I do."

We chatted for a minute longer, and then I got in the car to head home. The Clarks probably didn't have anything to worry about when it came to Karma. I was pretty sure she would come looking for me though.

When I got home, I suggested Hot Springs, Arkansas to Audrie since it was only a few hours away. She agreed. Everything was pretty much booked. We managed to secure reservations at the Embassy Suites Hot Springs Hotel and Spa. We left around noon, heading across the Hernando de Soto Bridge, into Arkansas. The drive was pretty quiet. I couldn't help feeling Audrie was still taking the situation out on me. After trying to make small talk and only getting short responses, I popped in a CD.

As we pulled up, I admired the scenery. The landscaping was beautiful this time of year. The flowers and their spring colors illuminated the place. Audrie seemed to perk up a bit. She reached over and rubbed my thigh.

"The first thing I want to do, baby, is schedule a massage at the spa," she said.

I pulled into a parking space. "That should help you to relax, sweetie. You want me to join you, or are you looking to do it by yourself?"

"Oh, baby, I would love for you to join me. Would you?"

I looked at her tenderly. "Absolutely."

She leaned in then kissed me. "Thank you for this trip, Cole. Thank you for being the kind, understanding husband you are to me."

I nodded then kissed her some more. Those words meant everything to me. She confirmed that my efforts to grow and be a better husband were paying off.

After checking in to our room, Audrie called to arrange our massage for the next morning, which was Sunday. She picked up a brochure in the lobby regarding a dinner cruise. It was a sunset dinner and dance cruise. It set sail on Lake Hamilton aboard the Belle of Hot Springs Riverboat. Audrie had me so hyped about spending time with her about the boat that I almost forgot the reason we left Memphis in the first place.

The Belle is a two hundred and fifty passenger boat that has graced Lake Hamilton since 1984. Audrie and I enjoyed the captain's narration as we received panoramic views of the Ouachita Mountains and other historical sites. Dinner was awesome, and so was our time on the dance floor. Audrie hardly wanted to sit down, but she changed her mind once she saw something peculiar. She abruptly stopped dancing.

"Cole," she said, holding my arm. The look on her face made my stomach turn. "It's her."

"What? Karma?" I asked, doing a 360 degree turn. "Where?"

Audrie was frozen. Her eyes were glued in the far right area of the boat. I turned in that direction, but I saw no one who resembled Karma.

"Sweetie, where is she?"

"Over there, Cole. She saw me looking at her, so she turned the corner, heading toward the stairs."

"So, she just went to the upper deck?"

"Yeah," Audrie answered almost in a whisper.

I could feel her trembling as I pulled her close. I swallowed hard. I didn't know what we should do. We were out in the middle of Lake Hamilton, and the cruise wasn't even half way through. The world went on around us. Happy people danced and sang along with the song the DJ played while Audrie and I stood motionless and full of anxiety. There was nowhere to run. I broke our embrace.

"Audrie, are you sure?"

"Yes," she answered.

"Sweetie, I need you to be sure you saw her because I'm about to have a talk with security."

"Go!" she yelled over the music. "Go talk to them, Cole! I'm sure!"

I inhaled then released a deep breath. I couldn't believe this was happening. Karma followed us all the way to Hot Springs? This is unreal. "Listen, sweetie. Go over to our table and have a seat while I talk to them."

"No, Cole. I want to go with you. I know what she has on."

"Okay," I said, grasping her hand. "Let's go."

We made our way across the dance floor and over to where a security guard sat. He saw us approaching, so he stood. "Good evening," he said. "May I help you?"

I couldn't believe what I was about to say. "Um, yes. My name is Colby Patterson, and this is my wife Audrie. Um . . . I don't know if you heard about the woman who broke out of the mental institution about ninety miles outside Memphis, but um . . . well . . . see um—" the words wouldn't come out.

"She's stalking us," Audrie came out and said.

The security guy looked as if he wondered if Audrie herself was crazy, and what did that have to do with him. I interjected.

"Sir, she's on this boat," I said. His eyebrows rose. "My wife just saw her. Apparently, she followed us here."

"Ma'am, you saw her?" the security asked.

"Yes. She just went to the upper deck. She is me-dium-complexion, wearing a black fitted dress, and she has long hair."

I stared at Audrie suspiciously. Karma whacked all her hair off before she was caught and sentenced. I doubted very seriously that she had long hair in a year. Audrie looked back at me.

"What?" she asked.

I started to question what she said about Karma's hair, but I refrained. "Nothing."

The security guy called for another officer. Once the officer came over, the first security guy explained the situation. Audrie stood, clinging to my arm until they finished talking.

"Okay, let's go see if we can spot her," the first offi-cer said.

We all headed to the upper deck. Audrie held on to my arm once again after we made it upstairs. We stood, combing the room with our eyes, looking for a lady with long hair and a black dress. Security asked us to stand back while they walked the deck. We agreed.

"How much time do we have left on this boat?" Audrie asked me. "I want off."

"Sweetie, we still have at least a couple of hours to go. The boat just turned around."

"Then, what are we going to do?"

"Listen. Karma can't do anything to us on here. What is she going to do? Attack us then jump off the boat and try to swim to land?"

Audrie and I began to bicker. She was clearly agitated, and so was I. A couple of minutes passed by the time security returned.

"Ma'am, do you see her because we haven't seen anyone fitting the description."

Audrie looked over the room then pointed. "There . . . heading to that corner."

When I looked where Audrie pointed, I saw a glimpse of a woman dressed in black, turning the corner. Security began to move.

"She's heading to the lower deck. Let's go," one of them said.

We all moved quickly to the other side of the deck—to the staircase on that end. Security was ahead of us. Once down the steps one of the officers was just inches behind the woman. He grabbed her arm, and she spun around then looked him up and down. Before he could say anything to her, she made eye contact with me. My rapid heart beat slowed then damn near came to a complete stop.

"What the hell are you doing?" she asked him just as Audrie and I walked up.

I looked at Audrie. She looked back at me. The officer said, "Ma'am, do you have some ID?"

The whole room seemed to have stopped, and all eyes were on us. I was embarrassed, and reluctantly I spoke up. "No need, sir. That's not her."

The officer turned to face me. "Excuse me?" he said.

"Don't bother with ID. I'm very sorry, but that's not her."

The officer looked at Audrie as if he wanted an explanation, but my wife dropped her head then ran off to the restroom. I faced the woman.

"Ma'am, I apologize for the mix up. My wife thought you were someone else."

The captain walked over, and so did the woman's husband. He was very upset at how security handled his wife. I apologized profusely and offered to buy the couple drinks, but they declined. The captain offered them tickets to take the cruise again on another day, and they accepted.

I looked toward the women's restroom. Something told me it would be a lonely rest of the cruise for me. I had a strong feeling Audrie would not be exiting until we made it back to dock.

Karma

8

I paid the cab driver another fifty dollars after he took me to a First Tennessee Bank where I wrote a check for two thousand dollars, payable to CASH. The teller asked for my ID as I knew she would, but by this time, identity wasn't an issue. Before stopping off at the bank, I detoured to a Golden Beauty Supply Store and bought a long wig with the Chinese-cut bangs to resemble the chick I stole the ID from. I looked damned good—better than her on the photo, I must say. The teller didn't even blink twice after glancing at the ID then handing it back to me. The only question was whether the account actually had two thousand dollars in it. It did. The teller kindly hinted about the balance.

"Ms. Tyler, would you like your balance on your receipt?"

"Um, yes. That will be fine. Thank you."

This female not only printed the receipt with the balance, but she also circled the amount at the bottom. Thank goodness I didn't try to get more because I would've been thoroughly embarrassed. I must've taken all of Robin Tyler's bill money. She only had eighty-four cents left. *Damn*, I thought. Lucky for me, this was a pay weekend for most jobs, or else she might not have had the two grand in the bank. The teller counted the cash out to me swiftly. I could hardly keep up. Excitement rose in me with the flash of each green bill as it slapped the countertop as she counted.

"Eighteen, nineteen, and twenty makes two thousand," she said then stuffed the money into an envelope. "Is there anything else I can do for you, Ms. Tyler?"

"No, ma'am. I answered. Thank you. This will be all."

I took the envelope, walked around the security officer at the door then hopped in the cab. We were off to my new home at an extended stay hotel. As we drove, I saw a string of strip joints. Suddenly, I knew how I would make my living until Cole and I were a family with our child. Stripping would keep some money in my pockets, and I could even save for a car. *Still young—with a hot body—why not?* I thought.

The driver took me to a place called Value Place on Winchester Road. At first glance, it looked fairly new. The driver stopped in front then offered me his number in case I wanted to call him again. I nodded and smiled. A personal driver was a great thought. I asked him to wait until I decided if I wanted to stay at the hotel.

Once inside the hotel, I was sold. The manager showed me a studio, which was all I needed. It was only one hundred and seventy-nine dollars a week, and it included a full-sized bed, a dresser and nightstand, a dining table with two chairs, a cozy sleigh chair, and a color TV with cable. That wasn't all. There was a full kitchen with a full-sized refrigerator and freezer, a two-burner stovetop, a microwave and plenty of cabinet space. The hotel even had an onsite laundry room. This was definitely my new home. I went back outside to let the driver know I would call him later, if I needed him.

I took my few bags and went into my new studio. I turned on the TV, looking for some news about my escape. I didn't see anything. I knew that didn't mean no one was looking for me. In fact, I was pretty sure Cole and everybody who had his back wouldn't rest until I was back behind bars—or, at least at the mental hospital. Why everyone had it twisted, I just couldn't understand. I've been a lot of things, but crazy—not at all. I just needed people to stop pissing me off. Cole knew I loved him. I just needed to get close to him one time, so he would remember the love we once shared. I put it on him good, and he knows it. He had to have missed me like I missed him. My panties got wet every time I thought of riding his thick, hard muscle between his legs. Too much time passed without me having my man. I want to get to him fast, but I also had to pace myself.

Before the sun went down, I fixed myself up. I put on a skimpy outfit I purchased at the beauty supply store. It was a pair of white leggings with silver dollar-sized holes in them. The top was also white and fitted, and it hung off one shoulder. I accessorized with a silver handbag and shoes, and I purchased a pair of fake Paparazzi-style earrings. The whole ensemble was cheap, and that's just how it looked. But it was the best I could do for the moment.

I called the cab driver to pick me up. He said he was off duty, so I had to call the cab company to send me another driver. I secured all my money, except a hundred dollars, in case housekeeping decided to come into my room while I was gone. It only cost me seven dollars and fifty cent for the entire cab ride to The Sable Foxx, one of the adult entertainment clubs I saw on the ride over to the hotel.

There weren't many cars outside. I wondered if this was the place I should choose. I paid the driver then got out of the car. A couple of men, leaning on a car in the parking lot, whistled for me to come over.

"Hey, baby, where're you going?" one of them asked.

"In the club," I answered.

They met me half way as I walked toward them.

"Naw, baby, you're not going to get in there," the same one with the low fade said. "Women aren't allowed in there without a male escort."

"Really? Well, then how am I supposed to apply for employment?"

The other one with the pretty, smooth goatee spoke up. "Oh, you wanna dance, baby? That's cool. My cousin owns this joint. Let me take you in to meet him."

Progress already, I thought. I was excited. We went inside the club with no problem. The bouncers asked me to stretch out my arms. They used the security wand on me and checked my small handbag before giving us clearance. I was led to the back and into an office where a heavyset, light-skinned guy named Big Mike sat behind a huge desk.

Low Fade tried to introduce me. "Hey, Big Mike, this is um . . . um," he said, snapping his fingers. He turned to me. "Oh, I never did find out, did I? Say, what's your name, sweetheart?"

"Robin," I answered.

"Robin what?" Goatee asked.

I drew a blank. I forgot the fucking last name. I just stared at him for a minute, trying to think of what to say next. They all looked puzzled, but then I figured how to answer. "I don't know if I want to tell you just yet. You'll know, depending on how this meeting pans out."

Goatee looked at Big Mike. "Hey, man, we just met her in the parking lot. She wants to dance. I told her I would bring her in here to meet you."

Big Mike fired up a cigar then fanned the guys away without saying a word. They closed the door behind them. He took a few puffs and sized me with his eyes. I waited for him to offer me a seat, but he didn't, so I started toward one of the chairs in front of his desk. That caught his attention.

He stopped me mid-squat. "Un-un. Did I tell you to have a seat?"

I stood up straight. "No, sir."

"What makes you think you can be a Sable Foxx? Have you ever danced before?"

"Of course I have," I lied. "I mean, it's been a while, and I've never danced at a place as classy as this one, but I know I will learn fast."

He took more puffs, exhaling long and deep between each. The room became cloudy, and I was pissed that my brand new wig was about to become home for the Stonewood natural sweet vapors. I ran my fingers through my hair. He motioned for me to take a seat.

"So, what if I start you on the floor first? I don't want to put you on my stage until I'm confident you are ready. My stage Foxxes are known for being showstoppers. I won't put you in the mix until I get some positive feedback about your private dancing."

"Alright," I said, nodding. "That's fair."

"When can you start?"

"I'm ready now!" I scooted to the edge of my chair.

He eyed me curiously. "Well, where are your clothes? I don't see a bag with you."

"I don't have anything else."

"So, you came to dance in that?" Now it was his turn to sit up in his chair.

"Well, I'm new in town, and that's why I need to get a job fast."

He waved his hands over each other. "Naw ... naw ... naw. Un-un. Ain't no way I can let you go out there like that."

"Please, Big Mike. I really want to start tonight. Just let me hang out then. I need to get a feel for what goes down."

He sat back in his chair and looked up in the corner as if he was thinking. "I tell you what," he said, turning back to me. "You're kind of small, but I've got some brand new outfits in the closet you can choose from. If you can wear any of them, I'll put you on the floor tonight."

"Oh, thank you, Big Mike!"

"Hold on . . . don't thank me yet. I'll have someone to show you the closet, but pay close attention to the price tag because it's coming out of whatever you make tonight. You will not get checked out of here until you at least make an attempt to pay on the balance for your suit."

"Checked out?"

"Yes. We hold your locker key and ID until all tips and debts have been settled."

This was a shocker, but what choice did I have. "Okay. I understand."

"Good," he said, picking up the phone. "I'll call Essence and Bunny to come show you the closet and give you the ropes on things." I nodded. "By the way, your stage name is Cookie."

Hell naw! I thought and almost said out loud. "Um, Big Mike, I'd like to come up with my own name, if you don't mind."

"I do mind. I have a system to keep all the girls' names from sounding the same. I'm back around to the letter "C," so unless you can come up with something I like, Cookie will be your name." He began speaking into the phone.

I thought like lightening—quick and in a flash. Somebody could wear the name Cookie, but it was not going to be me. As soon as he hung up, I said, "Well, I like Capri."

He puffed on his cigar. "Alright. That's cool. I like that," he said in a cloud of smoke. "Capri it is."

The ladies came to escort me. Essence was a tall, dark, slender woman with large breasts. I could tell they were real because she had on a bikini top, and her double-Ds bounced with every move. Bunny was a thick, white girl with copper-colored hair. She was bronzed by a perfect tan, and her ocean blue eyes gave her a striking look. I was a bit intimidated by these women, but I tried not to show it. I figured their money helped them to stay beautiful, so I had to make the paper, too. After looking at Essence and Bunny, I suddenly felt the need to pack on a few more pounds. Men love ass and titties, and Cole was definitely a man. Ten more pounds could only make him even more proud to be *my* man.

Cole

9

---

*N*early seven hundred dollars on a one-night, two day luxury getaway, and my wife ruined every moment. From the night cruise on the Belle, the fine dining the next day, the luxury spa treatments, and to the winery—Audrie was a wet blanket. She totally killed every experience with her horrible mood. I forgave her for the fake Karma sighting, and I let her know that, but she hardly spoke to me the entire trip as if I did something wrong.

Once back in Memphis on Sunday night, we picked up the children then headed home. I didn't appreciate how cold Audrie was when the Clarks tried to talk to her. She was short with them, and never once looked at them when they spoke to her. They probably thought she and I were having a fight. Now it was my turn to be pissed. The kids were half-asleep as I drove toward home. Audrie wanted to make a stop at the store.

"I'm out of razors. I need to stop at a Walgreens or something, unless you want me to use one of yours." This was the most she'd said to me in the past twenty-four hours. I had nothing to say, and she noticed. "Cole," she called. "Did you hear me?"

"I heard you," I said in short.

She huffed, apparently taken aback. "So, what do you want me to do? Use yours, or what? I need to get this stubble from under my arms before I wear my navy, shrug-sleeved dress to work tomorrow."

"I don't care what you do."

She huffed again. "Excuse me? Oh, so now you're not talking to me?" She got loud.

"Lower your voice," I said, my voice calm but deep.

"How dare you," she yelled.

I turned quickly to look at the children. They stirred a little. Shawna opened her eyes, squinting, seemingly wanting to know what was going on.

"Go back to sleep, Shawna. I'll wake you guys once we make it home."

Shawna lay her head over on her brother. I was confident she was instantly back to sleep because her breathing was heavy. As soon as I pointed my finger at Audrie and opened my mouth, nothing came out. I began to have vivid flashes of the argument Glenda and I had the night she was killed. Now, mixed in with my anger was pain. I couldn't do this. I bit my bottom lip—hard—and my breathing became heavy. Audrie looked scared. I lowered my hand then pulled over at the first chance. I turned on the emergency flashers.

I unfastened my seatbelt then picked up my wallet. "I can't do this," I said, opening the car door. "Take my children home."

Audrie frowned. "What are you getting ready to do?"

"I'm walking home. I need to clear my head."

I hopped out of the car then headed down the sidewalk. Audrie jumped out, too.

"Cole, are you crazy? What are you doing?" she asked, following me a short ways down the street.

I turned to her. "Get your ass back in that car with those kids," I said, pointing, my tone stern.

"Do you have any idea how long of a walk you have home?"

I stepped closer, pointing as I spoke. "Listen to me, and hear me good." She kept silent. "I'm too angry to get into that car with you right now. You have ruined what was supposed to be a wonderful getaway for us—"

"I'm not the one who slept with Karma and possibly made a baby—"

"I'm NOT finished!" I yelled, cutting her off right back. She stood silent with tears in her eyes. "I can't change the past! If you were going to keep holding the past over my head, you shouldn't have married me. Hell, I wouldn't have married you, if I had known you were going to do this!"

Her tears fell. "Cole," she said, her voice soft and filled with hurt.

"Damnit, Audrie . . . I . . . I—" I tried, but I couldn't fix what I said because I meant it. I lowered my voice. "Listen to me. I have a lot of things built up in me right now—possible paternity, Karma's escape, your paranoia, and now the argument with you in front of my children has given me flashbacks—this is all too much. I feel like I'm about to lose it."

"Well, let's just get back in the car—"

"No," I said, backing up. "Please, just take my kids to the house. I'll meet you there after I clear my head."

I walked off. Audrie called after me. "Cole!" she cried. "Cole!"

I didn't bother turning around. I was stressed beyond belief. I knew Memphis had a lot of crime, but this night, crime wouldn't want to duel with me. I had enough frustrations in me to really hurt somebody. I lost my first wife, whom I still loved, to senseless behavior, and now my current wife took me down a road I've been trying hard to get past. I loved Audrie. I married her because I wanted her to be a permanent part of my life. But, I also loved her enough to walk away. I was fighting mad, and no matter what, my wife didn't deserve to be on the receiving end of any type of wrath.

I heard the car moving slowly beside me, but I didn't turn to look. Audrie drove ahead a bit, but kept her speed slow. I could tell she didn't want to leave me, but my mind was unchanging. I wanted to be alone with my thoughts— sort things out. See if there was any way I could figure out how to fix all that was broken.

By the time I caught up to the car again, I still didn't look at Audrie. Obviously, she got tired of trying to get my attention because she picked up speed, drove ahead and didn't stop. I felt a sense of relief. I knew I probably wouldn't walk the entire way home, but I didn't bother to let Audrie know that. I needed her to understand how angry I had become about how she'd been acting.

After about twenty minutes, I stopped at an Exxon and bought a beer. I drank it while I waited for the Yellow

Cab Company to send a taxi. I sat on the curb because I didn't want to run the risk of the police riding by and seeing me drinking in public. I went back in and bought two more beers once the first one was gone.

Audrie kept blowing up my phone. I answered a few times to let her know I was alright, but after the cab showed up, I turned off my phone. I asked the guy to hold on while I finished the last beer, and then I got in the car.

When I said I needed to clear my mind, I meant it. I didn't need Audrie trying to force me into talking about the situation at the moment.

My beer was gone. I kept trying to think of a place I could go to have a few more drinks before going home. As the driver got on I-240, a billboard about a new establishment caught my eye.

"Excuse me, sir," I called. "Do you know where that new spot called The Sable Foxx is? I've never been, and I think I want to go there."

"Yeah, I know exactly where it is," he answered. "You'll like that spot. There's nothing else like it in Memphis—nothing but class."

"Really? Hmm. My wife will be pissed if she knew I was headed to a strip joint, but hey, it's the only place I can think of where I can get a few drinks and leave my problems behind for a bit."

"Just be careful, man, if you're not a cheater. The Foxxes will have you drooling so bad you won't be able to return home in the same shirt. Then, you'll be caught for sure because how do you explain that to your wife?"

We laughed. I felt a tinge of regret for heading to The Sable Foxx without my wife's acknowledgement, but now was not the time to renege. I truly loved Audrie, and there was no woman on either side of the earth who could make me cheat on her, so watching a few asses shake wasn't going to hurt me.

The driver pulled up to The Sable Foxx, and then valet ran to the car and opened my door. I paid the driver then stepped out. The taxi driver honked his horn, threw up his hand to wave bye, and then drove off. I turned to the valet.

"Welcome to The Sable Foxx," he said. "Are you one of our premier guests?"

I stared at him for a second. He was a well-groomed white man, maybe late thirties or early forties, dressed in a burgundy-and-black tuxedo with black shoes and white gloves. I answered his question.

"Well, I'd like to think so since I'm a first-time visitor, but if you're asking if I have a membership, the answer is no."

"First-timer, huh? Well, then we have to give you special treatment no matter what. We certainly want to give you a reason to come back."

I chuckled a bit then headed toward the entrance. The entryway was lined with red carpet and dark-red velvet ropes. I was screened with a wand and then allowed to enter. The first stop was a pay booth, where I had to offer a credit card for a tab. The lady at the booth was very attractive and polite. She let me know there was a twenty-dollar cover charge, but it came with a two-drink pass. She had a smile bright enough to be on a Colgate commercial. She held my credit card and driver's license then called a waitress over to escort me to a table. I was led to a table close to the stage area with the number five on it. The waitress told me the woman at the booth had already recorded my table number in the event I needed to be reached regarding my credit card or some other matter. She took my drink order then left me alone to take in the scenery.

The taxi driver was right. This place did have class. The women were beautiful from wall to wall. I saw an array of complexions, races, ages and sizes—all dancing at tables and making conversation with the guests. I glanced up at the stage and saw two beautiful women—one Hispanic and one butter toffee African American—working the poles at each end. They synchronized to "Dance Like A Stripper" by M.E., each climbing their poles at least six-feet up, and then spiraling back down, head first. The room went into a thunderous cheer.

Though I sat at a small table by myself, as I looked around, I noticed the room had to be filled with at least one hundred and fifty men of all races. I glanced at my watch. It was a quarter till mid-night. I began to feel guilty about not calling Audrie, but I was in the wrong place to do so now. The waitress came back with my glass of Absolut and cranberry juice. I looked at the drink and thought about how I would feel in the morning, especially since I had to return to work. Before I could make a sound decision, the music was lowered, and the DJ announced that Tremaine

Bowman, Point Guard, for the Memphis Grizzlies was in the house.

Tremaine and his crew of about twelve walked through the club, throwing peace signs and upward nods as they headed toward the other side of the club and into an area that had a sign over it stating: PRIVATE VIPS ONLY. Shortly after that, a new group of women came from the back and made a beeline into Tremaine's territory. One of them caught my eye as she passed on the far wall. She had on a skimpy but sexy as hell, white cowgirl costume with a pair of erotic, thigh-high, white, stiletto-heeled boots. Her shiny, black hair hung midway her back, swaying seductively as she strutted across the room. I couldn't take my eyes off her. She was gorgeous. It seemed as though she moved in slow motion. I got the sense that I knew her from somewhere. Only moments had passed, but it seemed as though I spent half a day swallowing her with my eyes. Maybe it was the combination of the beer I had earlier and the Absolut that had me crazy.

I began to feel that somehow she could sense me looking. And she did. She turned and looked at me briefly as she entered the VIP area, but it was the double-take she did that told it all. She *did* know me. And I knew her.

Karma

10

---

*M*y heart felt like it was about to jump out of my throat. I began to shake uncontrollably. *He's here!* I thought. *My man is really out there. Or, is he?* I couldn't really tell. The dim-lighting made it hard to know for certain if that was Cole I saw, but I was almost sure. I needed to get out of that VIP area, so I could find out if that was Cole, sitting alone.

Big Mike put Essence in charge of showing me the ropes. The night before, I mainly gave the guests table dances and small talk, and I made six-hundred dollars during my shift—enough to pay Big Mike for the costume from the closet, buy another one, and still had money to take home. The one I wore this night was a white giddy up-girl costume. It was a cut-out teddy on the sides with fringed details at the top and bottom, accentuating both my cleavage and bikini line. The shoulder straps were silver-studded, and the same studs also lined my white cowboy hat around the center. I tied a hot pink and metallic silver scarf around my neck for color, and put on a pair of white, thigh-high boots that had a four and a half inch heel.

Although I wasn't the thickest or had the biggest ass amongst the other dancers, I knew I could turn heads with anything I wore because of my sex appeal. I was hot, and I knew it.

I needed to see Cole. The other girls began double and triple-teaming the guys in Tremaine's crew, but my mind was on the other side of that curtain. Essence was just about to go sit on the couch with two other girls and Tremaine when I pulled her away.

"What's up, Capri?" she asked, eyeing me strangely. "You don't look well."

"Um, Essence, is there a way that the club keeps up with who comes in here?"

"Yeah, why? Are you nervous?" She didn't let me respond. "Girl, ain't no need in being nervous about these men. All of their IDs are at the front booth, so if they start to act up, they won't get away too fast without the police knowing all their business."

"You mean everyone has to turn in their ID as they enter?"

"Girl, yes. Big Mike ain't having men in here who might clown us."

I went into deep thought. After hearing this news, I wanted to get out of there just that much more. I couldn't stop trembling, and Essence noticed. She rubbed my arm.

"Hey, calm down, girl, it's okay. Tremaine and his boyz are cool. We 'bout to get paid, too." She smiled and nodded at me.

"It's not that, Essence."

"What? What's wrong with you, Capri?"

I stood straight and crossed my feet, squeezing my thighs together. "I've got to pee?"

She twisted her lips, and her heavy lip gloss crinkled with the motion. "What the hell? Didn't I tell you to use the bathroom before you got out here?"

"Yeah, you did, and that worked for me last night, but I must've had too much to drink tonight."

"Damn, girl, you're going to get me in trouble. Big Mike don't play about his VIP guests, and he's going to blame me since I'm showing you the ropes."

This girl wasn't hearing me, so I had to take my acting ability to the next level. I started pretending it was about to gush out. "Oh, no," I said, squirming. "Oh, no!"

"Capri, please don't stand here and piss in front of these men. You can't hold it?"

"No. Essence, please let me out of here. I can't hold it any longer. I promise not to let Big Mike catch me."

She looked reluctant, but she eased the curtain back then asked the bouncer to step aside so I could get out. We let him know that I would be back shortly so he would let me back in.

Confident, the man I knew as Cole wasn't looking, I eased around the opposite side of where he'd seen me, and then sneaked to the front booth. The woman sitting there wasn't busy at all. She looked rather bored since no one was there to get checked in to the club. She also looked gullible, so I tried her.

"Um, excuse me," I said.

"Yeah," she answered, slinging her short brunette bob as she turned to look at me.

"Hi . . . um . . ."

"Hi," she answered back.

"Um . . . Um . . . what's your name?"

"My name?" she asked, stupidly with her hand on her chest.

"Yeah . . . you. What's your name?"

"I'm Peaches," she said.

A white girl named Peaches—really? Her tone was flat, and if I hadn't seen her with my own eyes, I would've sworn she was a black girl just by her voice. She sounded like "Peaches" from the hood. She had me speechless for a minute. Any other time, I would've questioned her about her upbringing to see if she was just a wanna-be-black girl, but I didn't. This was not the time to make her angry. I needed some info, and I needed it fast.

I tried not to stare at the back of the head of the man who looked like Cole. I didn't want him to turn and see me. He had already looked as if he knew who I was. I decided to ask Peaches about the man.

"Do you know that guy at table five?"

She glanced at the table then shook her head. "Naw. This is his first time in here," she answered. "But he did come over here to ask about you though."

I took a deep breath then exhaled to calm my nerves. "Did he say why?"

"He said you look like someone he knows."

"Did he say who?"

"Naw, and I couldn't give him any information besides your stage name. We don't do that."

"So, you told him I'm Capri?"

"Yeah, and honestly, that's all I know. Big Mike has all your other info put away."

74

"Alright . . . cool," I said, glancing back at the man's table. I turned to Peaches. "Um, is it possible for you to tell me who he is? I'm trying to find out if that's my dad's friend," I lied. "I haven't seen him in a while, and the last thing I need is for him to see me in here and tell my pops."

"Oh, snap," she said. "Well, yeah, I can look him up for you. We're holding his ID and credit card since this is his first visit."

She pulled out the card box for table five. I kept my eyes on the table to make certain the man wasn't watching me. He sipped his drink and paid attention to the pole dancers.

"Once he becomes a regular, we'll log his info into our computer system," she continued. She held up a photo ID and asked, "You mean this guy?"

My face could've told it all, but I did my best to hold it together. I wanted to answer, but my mouth became dry in an instant. It was Cole alright. I glanced at his table. I wanted to run to him, sit in his lap, and tell him how much I missed him, but I couldn't. We were so close, yet so far apart. I never imagined being in the same room with him so soon. This moment felt like a dream—a wet one at that. Cole looked good. Damned good. Peaches took me from my trance.

"So?" she asked. "Is this him?"

I let out a nervous chuckle. Hopefully, she couldn't tell. "Girl, yes, and I can't let him see me."

She gave me a strange eye with a twisted eyebrow. "Girl, did you have a thing going on with your daddy's friend?" I didn't say anything, but I bucked my eyes at her, hardly able to believe she just thought of that on the spot. She smiled then sang, "Ooooooooohhh, girl, you a hot mess, aren't ya? What made you get with your daddy's friend? Oh, never mind. He is good-looking. I couldn't say I wouldn't do him either, and I'm sure his money spends just like the rest of 'em. Well, g'on, girl. You better get back in that VIP lounge before he spots you," she said, placing Cole's ID back into the box.

"Hey, may I see that one more time?" I asked. "I haven't seen him in so long. I just need to get a good look at his picture before I go."

She passed me Cole's license. He was definitely fine, but his picture wasn't the best-looking thing his ID had to offer—his address looked far better to me right then, and I was too glad. I memorized the street number and name then handed it back to Peaches. I eased her ink pen into my hand then thanked her for her help.

"You're welcomed," she said. "Now, hurry up and go."

I went back the way I came, grabbing a napkin off a table along the way. Once in the corner in the back, I stopped momentarily to write Cole's address on the napkin. I folded it and pressed it deep into my cleavage so no one could see. I tossed the ink pen into the corner then hurried back to the VIP area. I was certain Cole spotted me going back in, but I was too scared to turn and look before the bouncer sealed the curtains. Essence lit into me as I stepped inside.

"What the hell took you so long?" she said, damned near barking.

"Huh?" I answered. "I didn't think I was gone that long."

"Did Big Mike see you?"

"No, he wasn't even out there."

"Get your ass over to the couch, and don't leave this area any more tonight. You hear me?"

"Damn . . . alright. Calm down, hell."

That bitch didn't know who she was talking to, but this wasn't the time to show her. Good thing for her, I had just gotten some much needed information about my man's whereabouts, so I was in a halfway decent mood in spite how she had just talked to me. I went and stood in front of the couch then twirled my ass for Tremaine Bowman.

"Hey, now, sexy, where'd you come from?" he asked.

I didn't respond. I danced even harder. As I turned to face him, he was no longer Tremaine Bowman. He had become Colby Patterson, and his eyes were on me. We stared deeply into each other's eyes as I danced, and my mind went to places it shouldn't have. It felt like no one was in the room but Cole and me. First, his eyes undressed me, and then they made love to me. Nobody could help me now because I was on my way to the ultimate climax, and there was no stopping it.

Cole

11

---

*T*he taxi let me out in my driveway around 2:00 in the morning. I patted my pockets and realized I didn't have keys. I left Audrie with the car, and all my keys were on the same ring. I looked at my phone and refused to turn it on. I knew there would be a number of texts and voice messages left by Audrie that I just didn't want to deal with.

I stood in front of my door, contemplating whether to ring the doorbell or just sit on the porch. To my surprise, the front door opened. I stared into the saddened face of my wife as she stood, holding the door for me with red, swollen eyes. It was at that moment that I hated myself. I should've at least accepted a call or two from her, but I couldn't let her know where I was.

She looked me up and down then stepped back to let me pass. She fastened the door. I stopped midway the living room then turned to look at her once more. She seemed to be waiting for me to speak. I had nothing to say, so I headed for the bedroom. Her soft whisper stopped me.

"Really, Cole?" She wiped her falling tears and continued to speak in a hushed tone. "You leave me and the children here to worry about you all night, and once you come home, you have nothing to say to me? Really?"

I walked closer to her. "Audrie, I just needed to clear my head, and I really don't feel like talking right now."

"Cole, wasn't it you who said we would never again go to bed without first clearing the air? I've waited up for you, and I can't hear an apology or anything?"

"What? Wait a minute," I said, trying to keep my voice down. "Listen, I spent a lot of money, hoping to have a wonderful weekend with you. Not only did you ruin it with your paranoia and funky-ass attitude, but then you got shitty with me in front of my children."

Her voice rose a bit. "*Your* children? I'm your wife, Cole, and the only mother they know now, so I think that classifies them as *our* children."

"True. I didn't mean it like that, but—"

"And for the record, a crazy bitch just had a baby for the man I married. Now she could be coming to claim what her sick mind believes is hers. I reserve the right to be a little paranoid, don't you think?"

She doubled over and cried uncontrollably. My heart ached. I pulled her up then comforted her in my arms. "Audrie, we've got to believe everything is going to be fine."

"Oh, yeah? How can I believe that when the news reports are saying she's still out there? I can't rest until she's caught."

Once again, I thought of Glenda and how I ignored her feelings. I couldn't ignore that Audrie's concerns were valid, but there was no way I could change what was done. I held her in my arms for a bit and stroked her hair. After she calmed down, we headed for the bedroom. Audrie was dressed for bed, but I needed to take a shower.

Once in the bedroom, I kissed Audrie long and hard. "You're right, sweetie," I said just after breaking our kiss. "I do owe you an apology. I didn't know how to handle my anger tonight, and I'm sorry."

"I'm sorry, too, baby. I realize this situation has got to be stressful for you, too. I don't mean to add to your frustration." She placed a small peck on my lips.

"So, we're good then?"

She smiled and nodded then responded with another kiss. I went to take a shower. Several thoughts came over me as I relished the steaming vapors—my weekend, the blow up with Audrie, and then the woman in the cowgirl costume at The Sable Foxx. She was absolutely stunning. She was also familiar. The woman at the front desk said her name was Capri, but I was almost certain that could only be her stage name. She definitely knew me. Her eyes said it all. As the hot water ran over my head and massaged my back, the muscle down below became erect. I quickly bathed then jumped out of the shower.

Audrie was fast asleep, but I was too aroused to leave her laying there. Still wet, I rolled her off her side then spread her legs. She must've sensed I would be coming for her because she was naked under her gown. She fussed a little though.

"Eew, Cole, you're still wet."

"I know," I answered, running my hand up her stomach and to her breasts. "I want you so bad."

I pulled the gown over her head then entered her with strong thrusts. She moaned as I worked vigorously to go deeper and deeper into her mass. The erotic sounds off her lips kept taking me there. I wanted to release, but not without pleasing her first. I jumped off her, and then turned her over and gave her more long strokes. She was pleasantly surprised.

"Damn, baby, what's gotten into you?" she asked. "I love the way you're taking me tonight."

She backed that ass up to me, and damn, I wanted to release. She needed to get hers and get it fast.

"C'mon, sweetie," I said. "Give it to me. You feel so damn good, girl."

"You want it?" she asked softly.

"Yes," I whispered.

"You sure you want it, baby?" she asked again, throwing her voluptuous chocolate ass into me.

"Hell yeah. Give it to me, baby."

"Okay. Here it comes."

Her warm, wet walls contracted around me, sending me into a wild wave of pleasure. I couldn't hold it anymore. She lay on her stomach, trembling and panting while holding the weight of me. I wanted to roll off her, but at the moment, that wasn't an option.

"Thank you," she whispered.

"For what, sweetie?"

"For bringing that home to me."

I muscled the strength to roll off her and looked her in the eyes. "What does that mean?"

"Cole, I tasted the alcohol on your breath before you got in the shower. I know you went somewhere to have some drinks, so I'm just grateful you're the type of husband to come home rather than get with the first willing slut. If I know you correctly, you were in some whole-in-the-wall joint, and some woman was all up in your face."

"No, love. I sat alone, but I did have some drinks."

"I know you did. As a matter of fact, your breath is still strong because you haven't brushed your teeth."

"True. I intended to once I got out of the shower, but I couldn't think straight. I wanted you so bad."

She rolled on her side to face me. "So, where did you go?"

"Huh?"

"I didn't stutter, baby. It's a simple question. Where did you go?"

I felt another argument coming on. I had hoped she wouldn't ask, but now that she did, I couldn't lie to her. "The Sable Foxx."

"What?"

"The Sable Foxx. That new strip clu—"

"I know what The Sable Foxx is. Cole, why would you go there?"

I rubbed her arm. "Sweetie, I just wanted to go somewhere with music and to have a few drinks."

"All the hole-in-the-wall joints in Memphis, and you couldn't think of a place to go besides the strip club? Here I am worried about some woman in your face at a nightclub, but little did I know you were around plenty of pussies."

"Audrie, it wasn't like that. I didn't accept one dance from those women. I only had a few drinks. You can check my credit card receipt in my pocket, if you want."

"Oh, they're accepting credit cards for lap dances now?"

"Naw, woman. You know what I mean. C'mon now. Please let's not have a feud before we go to bed."

She poked her lips then said, "Well, again: I'm glad you brought it home to me."

"Wouldn't want to give it to anyone else. That's why I married you."

We shared a slow loving kiss. Audrie pulled back then asked, "So, did those women have anything on me?"

"Hell, naw!"

We both laughed.

"You better had said that." She laughed some more. "C'mon now. Really. There wasn't one woman who caught your attention?"

"Sweetie, I'm telling you. That's not why I went there. Only one woman caught my attention, and it wasn't because she was so beautiful," I lied. "I only gave her a second glance because she looked familiar."

"Really? So, how do you think you know her?"

"I think she's the new assistant in my office."

"Oh, really? I haven't met her. You mean the one who came just after I transferred to the other office, right?"

"Yeah, but it was hard to tell if it was really her because she had on heavy makeup and a hat, but I'm almost positive that was her."

"Wow. Did she see you?"

"Yes, and she knows I saw her, but she got by me because she had to go into the VIP lounge with Tremaine Bowman and his posse."

"Tremaine Bowman? Hmph. I bet she was glad of that. I hear those sport figures spend a ton of money in those places."

"Yeah, I'm sure. I won't say anything to her at work in the morning unless she says something to me."

"That's a good idea. You never know why she's working in a place like that. You don't want to embarrass her."

"Right. And speaking of work, we need to get some sleep. We only have a few hours left before we have to get up."

"Goodnight, baby," Audrie said then kissed me. "Oh, you might want to brush your teeth first. If you wait till morning with that breath, your teeth my rotten out."

We laughed, and then she turned over and backed up to me. I swung my arm over her waist and held her close.

I hated to lie to Audrie about how the assistant caught my eye, but she certainly wouldn't be able to handle that truth.

Karma

12

---

*T*remaine took six of us back to his hotel suite after our shift. Essence, Bunny and I were among those chosen to take the luxury, stretch Hummer ride downtown. Tremaine and his gang waited for us to shower and get changed after our set was over, so I borrowed Bunny's car to go to my hotel real quick. I made just over a grand in the VIP area, and I didn't trust leaving it behind in my locker. Once at my hotel, I changed into an outfit I bought that morning. I rocked a sexy pair of dark-denim skinny jeans and a bright-yellow, lace halter with nothing but a pair of hot-pink, heart-shaped pasties over my nipples.

When I got back, everyone was about to load up in the stretch Hummer, about to kick off phase two of our money-making tryst. Tremaine pulled me onto the seat next to him. He was all up on me. He was so close, in fact, that it was hard to lift my champagne flute to my mouth for a sip. The money I made at the club was the only thing keeping me focused. I knew there was more where that came from.

We cruised down Union Ave. I looked out the window as we approached Fourth Street, and I could see the

Fedex Forum. All of downtown was lit, and the scenery never looked more beautiful to me. I'd been locked up so long, I forgot what the rest of the world had to offer.

I glanced over at Tremaine as I sipped the remaining alcohol from my flute. He was a good-looking guy, but he was too young. The men in my life had to be at least twice my age, and besides, there was only one man for me, and that was Cole. Tremaine's drunk ass talked all the way to the hotel. I learned more about him than I cared to know.

"Yeah, if you were my shawty, I'd serve you this ten-inch dick every night," he slurred in my ear.

I rolled my eyes. "Really?"

"Believe that." He raised his glass to his lips then took a sip of his drink—the Remy Martin he and the fellas passed around. He turned to me and the smell of his breath burned my nostrils as he spoke. "You got off back there at the club, didn't you?"

"I don't know what you're talking about."

"Yes, you do. I saw you, shawty. You came hard, too." He chuckled.

"No, I didn't," I lied. "Why would you think that?"

"Yes, you did. I study women's faces when they cumming. You tried to play it off, but I knew the score. You landed one. I was that tempting, huh?"

I wanted to say, "Nigga, please. I saw my man's face when I was looking at you." But, I didn't. I turned away instead. He turned my face back to his.

"Shawty—"

"The name is Capri," I snapped.

"Okay, well, then, Capri."

"Yes?"

"You want some of this, don't you?" he asked, squeezing between his legs.

As I noticed his hardness, my eyes were glued to him, and I became moist. It seemed he was right about his size. I definitely wanted to see it. I couldn't stop staring. Tremaine grabbed my hand and placed it where his once was.

"It's big, isn't it?" he asked. "It's real. You wanna see it?"

I laughed. "What? You're gonna pull it out right here?"

"Naw. Hell naw," he said, frowning. "I'm talking 'bout a private show."

This was my cue to cash out. "Sure, but my private shows cost money."

He pushed my hand away. "What? You think I don't know that?" I didn't respond. He glanced down to my nipples. "Them damned things is pretty. You gon' let me suck on 'em?"

"Look, how long are we going to be kickin' it with y'all?"

He looked up and down the length of the stretch Hummer. "Sheee-iiiitt! Fuck them niggas," he said with a wave of his hand. "I'm talkin' 'bout me and you. I don't care what they doing."

"Well, how long do you want me tonight?"

"Till daylight."

When I made it back to the club before we left, it was around three A.M., so it had to be well after that as we rode downtown. I wondered if he even had a limit. I figured I'd try him to see.

"Three G's," I said with confidence.

"What the—" he said, sitting straight up, spilling a small dose of his drink over his hand and onto his jeans. "You've got to be kidding me." I stared at the wide-eyed glare he gave me. "Shawty, that's about a thousand dollars per hour."

I didn't back down. "I require seventy-five percent up front and the remainder before I leave."

He slowly lowered his glass to his knee without taking his eyes off me. "You better be fucking good, too."

"I am."

He had me nervous for a minute. I thought the awkward look on his face meant he was about to cuss and then throw me out on my ass. My nervousness turned into energy. I was ready. My plan was to rock Tremaine's world, so I could buy me a car. If I was going to keep up with Cole, I needed my own set of wheels, and the three thousand along with all the other money I'd made and stolen was a hefty start toward my goal.

Tremaine took me straight into his bedroom while everyone else remained in the living room of the suite. He ordered me to undress.

"Peel off them clothes, shawty, then get up on that bed until I come back."

He left the room for a few minutes, and when he returned he had a stack of money in his hands. He began placing big bills on the bed in front of me as he counted. I collected each stack of one thousand as he finished. He went into the bathroom, and that was my chance to find a place to stash the money until we were done. Such place didn't seem to exist, so I put the money inside the plastic laundry bag from the closet and hid it inside the leg of my jeans before folding them. I sat my clothes neatly in the chair next to the bed.

When Tremaine returned, I lay on the bed, spread eagle. He must've readied himself while in the bathroom because he was long and hard as he came toward me.

"You ready for this?" he asked.

My mind drifted, and I saw my man climbing on top of me. "Yes, Cole, I'm ready."

"What?" he asked, lifting his body to look in my eyes.

"Um, um…nothing." I couldn't believe I let that slip. "I was just saying I'm *cold*, but I'll be alright."

"Well, here," he said, pulling on the covers. "We can pull the comforter over us."

"No, I'm fine. Really, I am."

"A'ight, shawty, 'cuz I was about to say I'm 'bout to warm you up anyway. Slide yo' ass up some. You 'bout to get all of this."

That's what I want, Cole, I thought. I had it under control now. Tremaine pressed his weight on me, but it was Cole's body I felt.

Cole

13

I was at the facility for DNA testing by 9:00 A.M. Monday morning like the letter stated. As I sat waiting for my name to be called, I racked my brain, trying to remember if there could really be a possibility of me being the father of the baby Karma had. It didn't seem likely, but then again, she was supposed to have an abortion. So, the only thing I could come up with was that she didn't and that was the baby she gave birth to.

I never meant to do this to Audrie—the hurt, the pain and the aggravation of having to deal with Karma all over again. But what was I to do if the child was mine? I never thought I'd father a child outside my marriage and not raise him or her in my home. This child would be my blood and deserved to know me—to have my love and guidance. Somewhere there was a baby girl being cared for in a foster home who could possibly be mine. I didn't tell Audrie, but that bothered me—a great deal.

I sat, thinking for several more minutes, and then the nurse called me. "Mr. Patterson," she said, holding a clip board. "You can come on back."

I was well-past ready. It was time I knew some an-
swers. I stood then followed the long, blonde-haired
woman into a room. She asked me a few questions then
explained the process to me. I was extremely disappointed
to know the results would take at least a week to come
back. She stood and asked if I had any questions. At first I
said no, but then my friend, Nick, came to mind.

"Oh, I'm sorry, but I do," I said.

"Okay. No problem," she responded, sitting back
down.

"There is another possibility of paternity, but the
gentleman is deceased. Is there any way to resolve paternity for this child in this case?"

"Absolutely. If the father is recently deceased, perhaps he still has a toothbrush or some other article with his
DNA on it."

I shook my head. "Oh, no. He's been deceased for
quite a while, and I'm sure all of his belongings have been
discarded or removed from his relative's care."

"Okay. Well, there is always exhumation, but that
could be costly. The least expensive way to determine
paternity would be through relationship DNA—meaning if
his parents or siblings are still alive, they could be tested.
The closer the relationship to the alleged father, the better
the chances for accurate results."

This was great news because I had no idea this could
be done. "Great. I'll have to let his parents know."

I thanked her for the information, and she walked
me out. I had something else to think about on the drive to
work. What if Nick was the father? Did they sleep to-

gether within that timeframe? I wasn't sure, so I knew I didn't need to disturb his parents until my results were back. Perhaps they didn't need to know. Karma was more than a handful to have to deal with. How would this baby turn out as an adult?

I pulled into the parking lot of my workplace then got out of the car. It was a beautiful day, and my mood picked up since having gotten that DNA test behind me. I walked inside the building and spoke to the desk security officer.

"Hey, Tom. How's it going?"

"It's going great, Mr. Patterson," he replied. "You're running a little behind this morning."

I pressed my finger to my lips. "Ssshh . . . don't tell anybody," I teased, tossing him my morning paper as I strolled by his station.

"Thanks," he said, picking it up. "What would I do without you?"

I stopped and did a slow spin to look at him. "Um, you could cough up the seventy-five cents it costs to get one. That's what you could do." I laughed.

"Now why would I do that when I have your pockets to do that for me?" He laughed with me.

I shook my head. Tom was an older, graying white man—about sixty-four. He retired from the Memphis City School System, but after only a year in retirement, he applied for the security position at Essential Software Development because he felt he needed something to do.

"Enjoy your morning," I said just before jumping onto the elevator.

I heard him still laughing as the doors closed. Everyone knew I had my own schedule now that I had my former boss's job. Once the elevator doors opened on my floor, the new office assistant was the first smiling face I saw.

"Good morning, Mr. Patterson. I thought you weren't coming in today."

I stopped at her desk. "Aw, you should know better than that by now. You've been here long enough to know I put in a lot of hours."

"True. You are here a lot."

"I know," I said, reaching for my mail. "Even when I'm on vacation I seem to have to drop by this place for something or another." She smiled and gave me everything from my mail folder. "How are you this morning?"

"I'm well," she said. "Would you like some coffee?"

I stared at her for a second. She didn't seem bothered that I'd seen her in the club. She called my name, breaking my daze. "Oh, um . . . sure," I stammered. "Coffee would be great. I'll be in my office."

I walked off, hoping she didn't get offended at me staring. It would be hard pretending I didn't know about her secret life. She saw me at The Sable Foxx just like I saw her, but she was refreshed, bright-eyed and seemingly unapologetic for what I'd seen.

I stepped into my office then pulled up my email on my computer. I scrolled through a few messages marked urgent then got my writing pad out of the desk drawer to begin a to-do list for the day. There was a knock at the door, and then it opened.

"Hey, that was quick," I said.

"Yes, I already had a pot brewing. I needed some myself," she said.

My eyebrows rose. "Really?" I asked, reaching for the coffee. "Late night?"

She smiled slyly then shrugged. "Well, not really. I mean, it's nothing I'm not used to. I've been up a lot later, and then had to come to work before."

She had my undivided attention. I wondered if she would confess. "Is that right?" I sipped my coffee. "Mmm, this is tasty, Robin."

"Thank you," she said. "I figured I'd get your coffee right at some point or another."

"Yes. It's very good. Now, where's your cup? This is your long day to be here, right?"

"Oh, I'm going back for my cup. Yes, I'll be here until seven, so I can be off Friday. I never really thanked you for working out my schedule this way, did I?"

"Well, if you count saying thank you, I'd say you did."

She stood smiling. I began to have flashes of her at the club. The lady standing before me was a bit shy and reserved, but her personality at the club hot, sexy, alluring and seemed to be that of a woman with much confidence. All I could do was smile back, hoping to mask all the thoughts running through my mind.

"Well, I'm going to let you get your day started," she said, turning to leave. "Call me, if you need me."

"Thanks, Robin. I will."

When she left, I let out a deep breath. I couldn't tell if she was flirting, and being her boss, the last thing I needed was for her to think I was flirting with her. After more thought, I realized she might've hung around to feel me out—to see if I would admit I'd seen her. We didn't need to get into a discussion about the club, so I'm glad she didn't bring it up either.

After spending five hours at the office, I called it a day. I planned to get an early start in the morning since I started late today. I called Audrie once I got in my car to let her know I was on my way home.

"Hello, handsome," she said after answering.

"Hey, sweetie," I said. "Where are you?"

"I just picked up the children. We're heading home. Where are you?"

"I'm leaving work . . . heading home also. What's for dinner?"

"Well, I took the chicken wings out of the freezer this morning. I was thinking we could have some cabbage and candied yams with it. You seem to like my cabbage, and you know how the children love my yams."

"Yes, and daddy loves the yams, too."

"Then it's settled. Cabbage and yams it is." I could hear the smile in her voice. "I need to run by the store to pick up the cabbage and sweet potatoes, so you may beat me home."

"You want me to go by the store?"

She giggled. "No, honey. The last time I sent you to the store for some potatoes, you picked the worse ones they had."

"A'ight. Just thought I'd offer."

"Thanks, babe, but we're good. We'll see you when we get to the house."

"Alright. Love you."

"Love you, too," she said then hung up.

Traffic was great, so it only took me twenty minutes to get home. I stopped at the bottom of the driveway then got out to check the mailbox. There were a few pieces of mail, including a small envelope from The Sable Foxx. Damn, that was quick, I thought. Good thing I made it home before Audrie. I couldn't believe they could mail me something in the same day, even if it was in the same city. I looked at the front of the envelope again. It was stamped with today's date by the post office.

I hopped back inside the car and pulled up to the house. The envelope from The Sable Foxx had me curious. I went inside then stepped behind the bar to fix me a drink. I set the mail down, but the piece from the club kept staring at me. After fixing my drink, I opened the letter. It was a V.I.P. offer to attend the club on Saturday. My mind raced back to Robin. The first time I went there was pure coincidence. I wondered how she'd feel if I showed up there again. I was her boss, for goodness sake. I shouldn't be entertaining hanging in places where she stripped.

I set the envelope and invitation behind the bar then took the rest of the mail to the box in the kitchen for Audrie to sort through. There was no way I could go back to The Sable Foxx, knowing Robin would be there. Or, could I?

Karma

14

*T*remaine gave me a cell phone, asking me to be on call for him. I didn't mind. In fact, I was thrilled. His money was long—just the source I needed to get me on the road to living large. I needed a car, and though I was tired, getting a ride couldn't wait another day. I was dropped off at the club by Tremaine's car service. I didn't want him to take me to my hotel because I wasn't ready for anyone to know where I was staying. I was still a wanted person, and I just couldn't risk someone recognizing me, and then turning me in.

I called a cab to take me to my hotel. It took me half the morning to find a car lot that would let me put two thousand down on a car decent car. I rode off the lot with a two-year-old Honda Accord. I wanted the new Acura, but the owner of the lot said he didn't think he could get it financed for me. I had to take what I could get as Robin Tyler.

As soon as I drove off the lot with my car, I went to the club to cook up a little surprise for Cole. I paid Peaches to help me. She gave me a VIP pass, and then used the company's Netstamp to add the postage. I was so excited because I knew this would make the mailing look legit when Cole pulled it from his mailbox. I thanked Peaches, and she thanked me for the large bill I gave her. I headed straight for Cole's house. I needed him to get my envelope as soon as possible—before he made plans for the weekend.

I went and found me a new wig. I didn't want to go around town in the same wig I danced in. That would make it too easy to spot me. I purchased a light-brown, shoulder-length, curly wig. It was cute and innocent-looking, and I liked the change.

I went to the library. I knew not to go to the one in Parkway Village. I wasn't sure if the Robin lady had come back there to report what I did. I went to the Whitehaven Library to get on the Internet. I wanted to find the address to Cole's job. I remembered the company's name and a round about way of getting there, but I wasn't sure of the exact directions or if he was even still employed there.

The Internet always proved useful. Not only did I find out Cole was still there, but I found out Audrie was at a new location. I would've loved to have seen Cole today, but it was time for me to pay the new Mrs. Patterson a visit.

I drove over to the Germantown site of Essential Software Development. I made it there just in time because I spotted her long-legged ass getting into her car. I followed her as she got onto I-385 then hopped on I-240, heading east. I wondered where she could be going, but I got my answer when she exited on Walnut Grove and turned into a childcare center. I pulled over in a parking lot across the street then waited for her to come out with the children.

Once she secured the children in the car, she headed down Walnut Grove, and I followed, keeping a few cars behind. A few minutes later, she pulled into the parking lot of a Valued Food Mart. I started to sit and wait on her to come out, but I decided I needed to park a couple of rows over and didn't want to miss her.

As she and the children walked into the store, my heart was overjoyed to see my babies. I missed them so much. I could imagine how happy we would all be once we were together again. I longed to tell them they had a little sister. I knew they would be excited. I lagged behind them, careful not to blow my cover. Gavin was a little taller, and he sounded so cute as he spoke. I listened from the end of the aisle.

"May we get some Fruit Loops?" he asked, standing on his toes to reach for a box.

"We still have some at home, Gavin," Audrie said. "Daddy wouldn't like it if I bought some more before we eat up the box at home."

"Daddy will be mad at us?" he asked.

"Well, I don't know if he'll be mad, but he certainly wouldn't like it if I spent money I didn't need to."

"That's right, Gavin," Shawna said. "Daddy said eat what we have at home first."

Hearing her voice brought water to my eyes. I knew my babies missed me. I just wanted to go and scoop them into my arms. I decided to tip their way. Audrie and the kids headed in the opposite direction. I watched her at the fruit and vegetables, picking over cabbages and sweet potatoes. Once she started toward me, I ducked onto one of the aisles. She passed my aisle then went toward the checkout stands.

I waited until she headed out the store then started behind her. The woman at the checkout counter called after Audrie. Audrie had left a bag.

"Ma'am, wait," the clerk called. But Audrie didn't hear her.

"I know her. I'll give it to her," I told the clerk.

"Thanks," she said.

As I headed out the door, Audrie was already at her car, placing the few bags inside. I caught her as she was just about to strap Gavin in.

"Hi, you left this bag back there."

She turned around, noticing the bag outstretch. "Oh, thank you. I thought—" she cut herself off just after looking into my eyes.

"You thought what, Audrie?" I smiled sweetly.

It took her nearly a minute to finally speak. "How the hell did you know I was here? Have you been following me?"

"Now, Audrie, I thought you knew me by now. You've got something that belongs to me."

"What the hell do you mean?"

"You know exactly what I mean. You've got my man and my children." She looked as if she didn't know what to say next. "I'm back to claim them, *bitch*. By the way, did you let my babies know about their little sister? She's absolutely beautiful, and they're going to love her."

"Bitch, you're crazy," she finally said in a low tone. "Stay the fuck away from us."

I stepped closer to her. "Or, what?"

That seemed to have scared her. She called for the kids. "C'mon, Shawna. Unfasten Gavin. We've got to go back in the store."

I gripped her arm. "Leave something else behind?"

She snatched from me. "Get your damned hands off of me," she yelled. She leaned inside the car. "Gavin, Shawna, let's go now!"

When she rose from the car, I reminded her of something. "I got rid of the first one, Audrie. I suggest you get your ass out of the way, or else I'll get rid of you, too. I'm Mrs. Colby Patterson! You hear me?"

Once the children were out of the car, they busied themselves toward Audrie. She must've startled them when she raised her voice at them because they rushed to her without even looking my way. She grabbed their hands, one on each side of her, then scurried toward the store. I heard her car alarm beep as she reset it.

I yelled to her. "Don't make me have this conversation with you again, bitch!"

I hurried to my car then got out of that parking lot. Audrie could've just pulled off, but she probably feared I'd follow her. What she should've already figured out is that I had her address and had been there. I left because I didn't want to be caught by the police. The last look on her face let me know she was definitely going to report seeing me. At least I had the chance to let her know what I wanted to tell her, and I meant it. If she didn't get the hell out of my way, she was definitely going to be sorry.

Cole

15

As I pulled into the store's parking lot, I saw several flashing, blue lights lined in front of the store. There were people just outside the store, talking, but I didn't see Audrie and the children. No matter how hard I tried, I couldn't seem to catch my breath. Audrie called me only five minutes before to let me know Karma had been at the grocery store and assaulted her. I dropped the phone, slid into my shoes then raced to the store, not knowing what to expect. The collage of police cars and their blue lights made it all so unreal to me. I wished I was dreaming.

I pulled in front of the store then jumped out, brushing through the crowd of onlookers. I finally spotted a police officer in the doorway.

"Excuse me," I said out of breath. "I'm looking for my wife and children. My wife was the one who called to report the assault by the woman who recently escaped from the mental hospital."

The officer nodded. "Right this way," he said, leading me into the grocery store. We stopped at an office near the front. "This is the woman's husband," he told another officer standing at the door.

The policeman stepped back and allowed me inside the room. Audrie jumped to her feet and hugged me before I could close the door behind me.

"Are you alright, sweetie?" I asked.

"I'm okay. I'm just so shaken," she responded with her head buried in my neck.

"I'd like to talk with you, Mr. Patterson," I heard the officer say.

I opened my eyes and saw my children sitting and watching us quietly.

"Hi, Shawna and Gavin," I said, releasing Audrie to go to them. "How are you guys?"

"Fine," they said in unison.

I hugged them then looked them over. They seemed fine—not a scratch on them. They didn't even appear as shaken as Audrie. I asked them to stay seated then turned to Audrie. She looked fine also.

"Where are you hurt, sweetie?" I asked her. "What did Karma do to you?"

"She sneaked up on me, Cole. I didn't even know she was behind me."

"Audrie, sweetie, I hear you, but what exactly did she do to you?"

She looked stumped. "What do you mean?" she asked, frowning. "She startled me."

"You told me over the phone that she assaulted you. I need to know what she did and if you're okay. Do you need to see a doctor, sweetie?"

Audrie just stared at me blankly. I couldn't figure out what was going through her mind. *Did the sight of*

Karma shake her that much? I wondered. In the moments of silence, our Hot Springs weekend — the fake Karma sighting — came back to me.

"Audrie," I called, trying to break her from her trance.

"What?" she snapped.

"That's what I'm asking . . . *what*, if anything, happened to you?"

She frowned even more and placed her hand on her hip. "Cole, are you doubting me?"

The officer interrupted. "Excuse me, but I still have some questions." I looked over at the officer. "Have a seat, Mr. Patterson."

I did as told, and Audrie sat in the seat next to me. "Yes, sir. What questions do you have?"

"Mr. Patterson, this is the store manager, Mr. William Thomas," the officer said, pointing at the gentleman standing next to the desk. I nodded. "Before I go into any questions, I just want to let you know that I'm only doing my job. We've gotten a number of false sightings of this Karma Jolley woman, so in order to alleviate spending unnecessary money, time and overusing manpower, I need to clarify some things first."

"Okay. I understand," I said.

"We've been discussing this incident with your wife, but there are no witnesses, and your children don't recall seeing a woman in the parking lot with them."

I turned to Audrie. She looked as if she was about to blow a fuse. "Are you kidding me right now? Is this really happening? You all are accusing me of lying?"

"No one is accusing you of lying, Mrs. Patterson," the officer said. "We just—"

"Pull the tape from the cameras since you don't believe me," Audrie said in a stern tone.

"Mrs. Patterson, we—"

"I don't want to hear it! Just pull the damned taped!" she yelled.

"Audrie," I said, glancing over at the children then back to her. "Watch your mouth and lower your tone."

She pointed at me. "You are not going to do this to me again, Cole. She was real this time," she said, her voice still elevated. "I saw her. I talked to her!"

"Audrie, I want to believe you, but you told me she assaulted you, but you can't even tell me what she did."

"She grabbed my arm! I had to snatch away from her!"

"Alright, alright…calm down, Mrs. Patterson," the officer said. "We're going to do as much as we can to help you feel comfortable again." He turned to the store manager. "Can we just pull the surveillance tape and take a look at the timeframe Mrs. Patterson was on the parking lot?"

The store manager shook his head. "No, I'm afraid not. The outside surveillance system has been down for two days now. We're still waiting for home office to get someone out here to fix it."

"Unbelievable!" Audrie said, flailing her arms. "Unfuc—" she stopped herself as she turned and noticed the kids watching. "Just unbelievable."

I interjected her bit of rage. "Look, let's just move on, so we can get our children home," I said. "What else can I help you with?"

"Your wife was telling me, before you came in, about this woman and who she is to you and your family."

"Okay, well, I'll do my best to catch you up to speed. Oh, just so you know: My wife and I asked for occasional monitoring of our home once we heard of her escape."

"I understand. Your wife told me. I've put in a call to verify that was done. I'm waiting for a response."

"Great," I said.

We were there, speaking to the officer, about ten more minutes, and then we got up to leave. Everyone seemed to be staring at us as we headed for the exit. On the outside, we were greeted by news cameras from every local station. They bombarded us with questions, wanting to know if my wife really had an encounter with the escaped mental patient and the details of what happened. We didn't tell them anything. I simply brushed them off.

"I'm sorry, folks," I said, escorting Audrie and the kids to her car. "My wife has had a trying day, and we're done talking right now. We've said all we needed to say to the police."

My statement didn't stop their questions though. We continued to ignore them as we drove off the lot and headed home.

Audrie made it into the house before I did. I heard doors slamming as I entered. The children looked puzzled as they stood in the living room. I assured them everything was fine.

"Did we do something wrong, Daddy?" Shawna asked.

"No, honey. Audrie is just having a bad day, but I'm going to talk to her in a minute. Everything is fine, so you don't have to worry, okay?"

"Okay," she said.

"Do me a favor and take Gavin into the kitchen for a snack. You have fruit cups in the refrigerator and cheese crackers on the counter."

"Okay, Daddy," she said. "C'mon, Gavin."

The children headed for the kitchen, and I headed for my bedroom. Audrie was out of her work clothes and about to slide on a pair of skorts with a tank top. She saw me enter the room, but she kept dressing. I sat on the edge of the bed, waiting to see if she would acknowledge my presence, but she didn't. After putting on her clothes, she slid on her house shoes then started out of the room. I called her, stopping her.

"Audrie," I said. "So, you're just going to act like you don't see me sitting here?"

She turned to look at me. "I see you, but I have nothing to say right now."

"Well, I do."

She shrugged. "Well?"

"Clearly you're unhappy right now, but that makes two of us, so we've got to talk about this before dinner?"

She closed the bedroom door. "Cole, you embarrassed me at that store. Those people think I'm crazy because they could hear it in your voice that you didn't trust me either."

"Audrie, you're overreacting."

"Overreacting? Cole, you weren't the one faced with that crazed maniac, and then was pretty much made out to be a liar by everyone."

"Sweetie, you have to put yourself in our shoes. Nobody else saw her—"

"Forget it," she said, throwing her hands.

I reached for her hand. "Audrie, let's call for another update. Maybe Karma has been captured, but we just don't know it. We haven't sat down to watch the news lately."

Audrie frowned. "You think I'm crazy, huh?"

"No, I don't."

"Cole, she hasn't been captured because I saw her this evening at the Valued Food Mart. She wasn't a ghost. She wasn't a figment of my imagination, or a hallucination. I have good damned sense, and I need for you to believe me."

I remained silent, looking into her eyes. She seemed to be telling the truth, but she'd seemed sincere in Hot Springs, too. I wanted to believe her. I just couldn't. She spoke again before I could.

"And to think that you just might have fathered a child with this maniac is just—"

"Audrie, let's not go there. We're going to remain hopeful that the baby isn't mine."

"Did you go take the paternity test, yet?" she snapped.

"I did—"

"And?"

"And I won't know the results for another week or so."

"Great! Something else we'll have to suffer through."

"Well, at least the test has been done, and a week really isn't that long. Who knows . . . perhaps we'll get the results sooner."

She huffed and stomped. "Cole, the way I feel right now, I would kill that bitch, especially if I knew I could get away with it."

"Don't say that, Audrie. You really don't want to kill anyone."

"She threatened me! You weren't there!"

"Ssshhh," I said, hoping the children hadn't heard her yelling. I had to say something to appease her. "Okay, sweetie. Then, we'll have to find her. I'll place another call to the authorities for an update and make sure they are monitoring our home. Meanwhile, you don't seem to be comfortable knowing she has been caught, so why don't you take a leave of absence? I'll send you to stay with your mother in Dallas."

She took a deep breath then released it before taking a seat on the bed. "You're right. I'm tired of ducking and looking over my shoulders already."

"We can make arrangements for you to leave in the morning, if you want."

"What about the children, who's going to—"

"They'll be fine. I'll get them to school—"

"And my job . . . I haven't called them."

"Call them while you're at the airport, if you have to. It's final, Audrie. You need to get away from here and be at peace for awhile." She nodded. "My job is to see to it that Karma gets caught and thrown in jail by the time you return."

She smiled then stood to embrace me. "I love you so much."

"I know, sweetie. I love you, too. That's why I'm doing this."

Karma

16

When I got out of my Honda Accord to go inside the floral shop, I knew I was looking good, and my reflection in the window proved it. My new wig, color number four, was sexy. I had a mind to go lighter next time. *Who knows? I just might even go blonde soon,* I thought. Audrie sure as hell had to look at me twice. The bitch didn't recognize me with the new hair and a few extra pounds after having the baby.

I could only imagine what my baby girl was doing. Since her birth, I haven't been able to hold her or even see her. I had some pictures, but that wasn't the same. I wanted a real connection—to be able to look into her eyes and sing to her as my mother did when I was little. Colbia was somewhere off in a foster home with people who weren't her blood, but all that would change real soon. She was about to have all of us in her life. That's right—Cole, Shawna, Gavin, and me. The day we could all be a family just wasn't coming soon enough. I needed to kick things up a notch.

I opened the door to the floral shop. A bell chimed, alerting someone of my entrance. A petite, older white woman stepped out from the back.

"Yes, ma'am," she said. "How may I help you?"

"Hi," I responded politely. "I need to order some flowers for someone and have them delivered early in the morning."

"Oh, that's no problem," the woman said. "Looking for anything in particular?"

"Uhm, yes. I think I want to do a dozen of red roses."

"Well, that's simple enough. Everybody likes roses." She picked up an order slip then asked for my name.

I didn't want to give her my name. I couldn't let the old woman know the "escapee" from the mental hospital had been there. At the same time, I needed for Cole to make no mistake about who had them delivered. I looked around the shop for cameras. I didn't see any, but that didn't mean there weren't any. I reached inside my purse then placed my sunglasses over my eyes. The woman eyed me suspiciously.

"Um . . . is . . . everything alright, ma'am?" she asked, her voice alarmed.

"Of course," I answered. "All is well. So, what's the earliest you deliver?"

"I can have them arrive by nine A.M."

"Un-un. I need them sooner."

"But ma'am, we don—"

Her comments were cut short when I placed two crisp one hundred dollar bills on the counter in front of her. She was totally distracted. "Keep the change," I said.

I saw her throat move when she swallowed before speaking. "How early do you want them there? I'll deliver them myself," she spat quickly.

"Awesome." I smiled. "Now, you won't need my name, but I do want to write a message on the card."

Getting the woman to agree with anything I wanted from that point on was easy. I was the only customer in the store, and from the looks of things, business had been slow. I'm sure those two large ones came in handy near closing time.

As I left the shop, the cell Tremaine gave me began to ring. I answered as I got into the car.

"Hello," I said.

"Shawty, where you at?" Tremaine said.

"Out and about. Why?"

"I need to see you."

Damn, didn't you just bang the hell out of me all night last night? I thought. "When?" I asked.

"How soon can you get here?"

"Where are you?"

"At home."

"Like I know where that is."

"Southwind."

"A'ight. Give me the address, and I'll be there in about an hour."

Tremaine waited for me to find a piece of paper and a pen. The best I could come up with was my eyeliner and a receipt for my new wig. I turned over the receipt then wrote on the back of it with the eyeliner.

"A'ight. I should be able to find you," I said just after he gave me the address and brief directions.

"Hey," he called.

"What?"

"Cancel all yo' plans . . . you laying low with me tonight."

"That's cool. I wasn't going to the club tonight anyway."

"Dig that."

We hung up. I thought about going back to my room to change, but then I looked down at myself. Hell I looked good in my cream-colored, one-shoulder fitted dress with snake-skinned, strapped sandals. I freshened my makeup then started the car. My phone rang again. *What does he want now?* I thought.

"Hello," I answered.

"Ms. Tyler?" a man asked.

"Yes?" I responded, apprehensive.

"Ms. Tyler, this is Doug Henson down at the car dealership.

"Yes, sir. Is everything alright?"

"Oh, yes, ma'am. I was just calling to see if all is well with the car."

"Yes, I'm enjoying it. I'm glad I stopped by today."

"Well, ma'am, I hope you don't think I'm prying, but I just have to ask if you're still employed with Essential Software Development."

"Excuse me?"

"Well, as I said it's not that I'm prying in your business. I just know that you really wanted that Acura, but you never disclosed your income from your other employment. When you came and applied for a car a few months ago, you were too new on the job then. We still have your profile, and I noticed you never mentioned Essential Software. If you still work there and have at least one check stub, I think I can get you approved to take that Acura home."

I was stumped. I couldn't believe my ears. *Did this man just tell me that Robin Tyler works at Essential Software?* I wondered. *Cole's place of business?* I knew I heard him right, but my mind was moving a hundred miles per hour. Had I really been so lucky to run into a woman who not only looks like me, but works at the same company with my future husband? Mr. Henson pulled me out of my daze.

"Hello? Ms. Tyler? Are you there?"

"Oh, um, yes. I'm here. I'm sorry, Mr. Henson. I would love to continue this conversation with you, but I'm in the middle of something. May I give you a call in the morning?"

"Sure. If you don't call me, I'm going to call you. I really think we can work out the sale."

"Great. I look forward to talking with you tomorrow."

My heart raced. Essential Software had two locations, so I needed to know which one Ms. Robin Tyler worked for. I could only hope she was in the same building with Cole. It was after business hours, so my next flight was to Tremaine's home. Ms. Tyler and Essential Software would wait till morning. Money was calling my name.

Cole

17

After dinner, Audrie and I watched a movie with the children, and then it was their bedtime. They took their baths, and then we let them know Audrie would be leaving town for a while.

"I want to go, too," Gavin said to Audrie.

"Well, son, I would love that," Audrie said, "but I think it would be a better idea if you stayed." She turned to me. "Aren't they supposed to visit with the Clarks this weekend?"

"That's right, son," I answered, turning to Gavin. "Did you forget your grandparents asked for you to spend the weekend with them again?"

"Oh, yeah," he said. "That's right. Grandma and Grandpa are going to take us to put flowers on Mommy's grave."

Audrie and I looked at each other. The Clarks usually included me on the cemetery visits, so I could be there for my kids. They hadn't mentioned this visit to me, so I was very surprised to hear Gavin say this. I tried not to be shocked or disappointed. I changed the subject.

"So, anyway, Audrie will be back soon. We will just take care of the house while she's away, right?"

"Right," Shawna and Gavin said in unison.

"Oh, can we talk about a getting a pet when you get back?" Shawna asked Audrie. "Both of you said we could talk about it next month, and it is next month—I think."

Audrie and I looked at each other and laughed. "Well, I don't know, Shawna," I said, thinking of the heartache they suffered when Karma killed Princess. I didn't want them to experience any more trauma with pets. "I guess we can discuss it when Audrie gets back, but don't take this as a yes to getting a pet."

"I want a baby brother," Gavin surprisingly stated.

I looked at Audrie. Her eyes were widened as large as mine. "Is that right?" I responded. "So, you thought you'd just spring that on us, huh?"

"Well, can't you just call the stork?" Gavin was serious.

"Um, son. Babies don't come from storks," I told him.

"Mm-hmm. I saw it in a book. Where else do they come from?"

He really seemed shocked. He waited patiently as Audrie and I searched the ceiling for words to fall into our laps. Audrie rescued me.

"Well, son, that's a conversation you and your daddy will have at a later date. But right now, it's your bedtime."

Audrie and I kissed them goodnight before retiring to our bedroom. She wanted to know if I would join her in the Jacuzzi, and I did. It was a joy to soak while the jets sent powerful waves of hot water over our bodies. Audrie lay on top of me while I massaged her lower back and plump, round ass. Her moans turned me on. The heat of my body began to rise underneath her. She moaned louder then covered my lips with hers.

"I want it," she said in between kisses.

"Take it," I responded, sliding her my tongue.

We made love in the Jacuzzi for nearly an hour. She gave me all of her, and I relished it. We weren't sure how long she would be away, so we needed to enjoy each other for as long as we could. She seemed to let go of all thoughts of Karma and what did or didn't happened that day. Our time was all about us.

The next morning, I called everyone involved with Karma's case. The mental hospital told me they were reporting every lead called in to them. The fugitive department with the Memphis Police Department gave me the same report. I also confirmed there was extra police monitoring around my home and my neighborhood. Audrie shrugged once I gave her the not-so informing news.

I took the children to school while Audrie packed and took care of last minute details. Once I returned, Audrie was in the kitchen on the phone with her mother, discussing her flight plans. I went into the bedroom to retrieve her bags and set them in the living room. I had just returned with final bag when the doorbell rang. I called into the kitchen and let Audrie know I would answer it.

I looked through the peephole and saw a man with some roses. I opened the door, thinking he had the wrong address.

"Hi," I said to him.

"Hello," he responded, looking at a note card. "Are you Mr. Colby Patterson?"

"Yes," I answered, stunned.

"These are for you." He handed me the roses and a note then walked off toward his delivery van.

I started to ask who had them delivered, but then I decided to read the card. It stated: dear cole, you still look good. in fact, good enough to eat. i can't wait to swallow you whole again real soon. yum! i look forward to us, including our new baby, sharing our lives as a family. miss you and love you lots!

After reading the note, I snatched the door open then went out on the porch to see if I could catch the delivery man. He was gone—without me having noticed the name of the company on the van. The note card was plain and intentionally void of a company's name.

As I stepped back inside, I heard Audrie's laughter as she finished the call with her mother.

"Yes, ma'am," she said from in the kitchen. "I look forward to seeing you, too. Tell everyone I said, I'll catch up with them tomorrow. The rest of the day will be just for you and me when I get there, Mom."

I panicked as I looked at the bouquet of roses. They were neatly housed inside a lovely glass vase. As Audrie's conversation came to a close, I knew there was no time to hide them.

"Okay," she said. "Love you, too. See you soon."

My heart thumped against my chest hard. I looked down and noticed I was still holding the note. I balled it up quickly then tossed it behind the couch in just the nick of time. Audrie stepped out of the kitchen, smiling.

"Where did you get those, babe? Who was at the door?"

"Um, these? Um, well . . . um—"

"Are those for me?" she asked, taking them from me. "Cole, they are beautiful, but I can't take them on the plane with me."

"Oh, I know, sweetie. I'm just going to leave them on the kitchen table for a while."

"But, honey, you shouldn't have bought me roses on the day I'm leaving," she said, picking up her purse from the couch. "You could have saved that money and just got me a card or something."

"You're right, sweetie. I don't know what I was thinking."

"I'll just take one with me all the way to screening at the airport. I'll probably have to throw it away at that point, but at least I can enjoy it until then."

I set the vase on the coffee table. "Great idea, sweetie," I said, my nerves getting the best of me.

I needed to get Audrie out of there. It was now clear to me that Karma was haunting us. Audrie had been through enough. I just couldn't bring myself to tell her Karma was behind the roses.

Audrie lifted the handle on her rolling, carryon bag near the end of the couch then said, "Baby, grab that other suitcase so we can—"

She stopped. Her back was to me as she stared down at something. She bent to pick it up. Once she spun around with the note I'd balled up, my heart fell. The paper must've rolled to the end of the couch as I tossed it over the back. I sat in the wing chair as Audrie read the message. When she finished, she sat on the arm of the couch with her shoulders slumped. I didn't know what to say, but soon she sure did.

"And here I was, thinking you were just so kind enough to order roses for me," she said. I didn't look up at her. I sat with my hand propping my head. "You were just going to let me leave here without admitting you finally had a real encounter with Karma, huh?"

"I didn't want to worry you," I said softly.

"What?" she yelled. "Speak up! I can't hear you."

"I didn't want to worry you, Audrie."

"Look at me!" I did as told. "I've been accused of being crazy—"

"Nobody accused you of being crazy—"

"Yeah, just short of it though," she said, cutting me off. "You better do something about her before I get back, Cole! I'm NOT going to continue living my life in fear of her. If she was the kind to face you head on, that would be okay, but Karma likes to catch you slipping—sneak up on you. Somebody's going to get hurt, Cole, and I'll be damned if it's me . . . nor will I lose my family."

"What is that supposed to mean? You think I want Karma?"

"Well, I would hope you don't want her, but that's not what I meant. I'm saying I refuse to stand by and not do anything until she hurts you or the kids."

"Listen. I know that girl is crazy. Don't you think I want her caught, too?"

She grabbed her purse and bag again. "Let's go. I need to get away from here as soon as possible. The longer I stick around, the madder I'm getting." She stormed toward the door then yelled over her shoulder, "Get rid of those damned roses!"

I grabbed the whole vase then headed straight for the garbage outside, so Audrie could see the deed was done.

Karma

18

---

*T*hat Tremaine was almost good in bed. Poor thing. He tried his hardest. He needed to learn to slow down and stop fucking like a rabbit though. When he took his time, he had potential, and I could somewhat enjoy it. He was even better when I imagined he was Cole.

I really didn't want to be there with Tremaine, but his money wouldn't let me say no. When I asked him for three thousand dollars to stay the night with him, he gave it to me easily. I told him I needed to get something out of my car before we got started, and that's when I took the money and hid it in my glove compartment. My car was parked on the street in front of the house because there were too many cars in Tremaine's driveway when I arrived last night. By the looks of things, I thought he was having a party, but once inside, I saw we were the only ones there.

"Where is everybody?" I asked him.

"Everybody like who?"

"There're at least six cars in the driveway."

"Oh," he laughed. "There're only five out there, but they're all my vehicles. I have some more in the garage. I need to build more garage space, huh?"

"You think?" I said, jokingly.

He gave me a quick tour of his place. The first floor had three bedrooms, the living room, kitchen, a cozy den and a theater room. He took me to the backyard where I thought I'd see a swimming pool, but I didn't. His backyard led straight to a full neighborhood golf course beyond the patio. I watched him fix me a drink once we were back in the kitchen, and then we headed upstairs.

There were three more bedrooms upstairs, but I didn't understand why Tremaine needed such a big house. *Is this what millions do to you?* I thought. *Make you spend money you don't really have to?*

Tremaine invited me inside the shower with him, and I obliged. I hated every minute of the shower scene, but I still put on a good show for him. As I gave him head, I reminded myself that I was only making a living, so I could survive until Cole and I could be together. I knew Cole wouldn't approve of the things I was doing with Tremaine. This was straight up prostitution, but what he didn't know wouldn't hurt him.

I lay in bed with Tremaine as he slept soundly the next morning. I knew he was tired. Hell, he worked hard enough for his money. I lay wondering if Cole had received my roses yet. I knew he would be shocked to get them, considering I'd never given him flowers before. This was a new day, and a new Karma. I was officially a mother now, and once Cole helped me find our baby, we were going to have a great life. The only thing was trying to figure out how I wanted to get rid of the Audrie bitch. I had some money thanks to Tremaine and my stripping gig. I could just pay someone to do it for me like I did with

Cole's other problem he called his wife. But there was something about Audrie that made me want to choke the life out of her myself. She had a smart mouth and would go for bad when she wanted. I still had time to decide though. I was taken from my thoughts when I heard something downstairs. I shook Tremaine.

"Tremaine," I called. "Tremaine."

He rolled over, "What's up, shawty?" His voice was low and groggy.

"You got a dog?"

"Huh?" he asked, squinting.

"You got a dog or some other kind of pet? I heard something downstairs."

"You heard something?" He rose on his elbows, squinting at me.

Just then, we heard, "Tré!"

His eyes widened, and so did mine. If he saw a need to be alarmed, I sure as hell did, too. He jumped up, scrambling for something to put on. I lay there naked as a jay-bird, so I jumped up, too.

"Who is that?" I whispered, combing the room with my eyes. I didn't see my dress.

"Tré!" the woman called again. "Are you up there?"

"It's my wife. Get in the closet," he demanded. "Hurry up."

His wife? I thought.

"Tré, are you up here?" Her voice was closer. She was obviously on her way up the stairs.

Tremaine gave me a pleading look. I hurried in the closet then stood, listening.

"Baby, what are you doing home? I thought you were gonna be in L.A. for two more days."

"I decided to cut my trip short, and good thing I did because you're up to your old tricks I see."

"What're you talking about, baby?"

"Don't play with me, Tré. Where the bitch at?"

"Huh? Baby, stop trippin'."

I heard a slap followed by Tremaine yelling. "What the fuck did you do that for?"

"I'm sick of your whoring ass! Just tell me where you stashed the bitch, so I can kick her ass, and then finish beating your ass!"

"Baby—"

"Shut the fuck up! Don't say shit to me unless you're going to tell me where to find your whore." Her voice trailed to another part of the room. "I'm tired of this shit! You think I'm fucking stupid, Tré? This ain't my fucking dress! I don't wear cheap shit like this! No wonder she left the shit on the stairs."

I rolled my eyes and shook my head. I totally forgot Tremaine peeled my dress off me as we headed up the stairs. He made me continue the tour in the nude, saying he needed scenery, too. The woman's voice came toward the closet, so I braced myself.

"I don't know why these bitches do this. There isn't a whore alive who don't know you're married."

I could tell Tremaine was close behind because his voice was near, too. "Baby, come here."

"Let me go, boy!"

The closet door slid open, and there I faced both of them.

"I knew your ass was in here, bitch!" she said. "Get your funky, naked ass out of my closet, stinking up my clothes!"

She yanked at my hair, not realizing it was a wig. When she pulled the wig with force, it came off, and she fell back on the floor. She scrambled to get up, but she wasn't quick enough. Tremaine held her down.

"Let me go," she screamed. "I'm going to pop a cap in her ass. Move so I can get my gun!"

"Go!" he yelled to me. "Get out of here."

"My dress!" I said.

He nodded his head in the direction of my dress. His wife must've tossed it onto the floor near the bed. I picked it up then slid it on. I ran down the stairs and to my car. I balled off, not looking back. Tremaine had me fucked up. He put my life in danger. That woman could've walked in while we slept in the middle of the night and shot us. That would've put a wrench in all of my plans with Cole. Tremaine hadn't seen the last of me, and that was for damned sure.

I went to my hotel to shower and change. I also needed to buy a new wig. This time I bought a short, auburn bobbed wig. I absolutely loved the new faces I could become. After leaving the wig shop, I drove to Essential Software then parked on a crowded row. My plan was to go inside and chat with the guard a bit, but before I could turn off my ignition, I saw "the" Robin Tyler, getting out of her car only two rows up from me.

I lowered my seat back a bit, and then put on my sunglasses. A car pulled into the spot next to her, she smiled then waved. She headed toward the building, but turned back when the man in the car rolled down his window and called to her. I cracked my window to see if I could hear what the conversation was about, but I couldn't hear a thing. She smiled again, heading back toward the man's car. He stepped out, and my heart skipped a beat. It was Cole! I could hardly catch my breath. The very sight of my man did things to me that nobody could.

Robin took what looked like a box of Krispy Kreme doughnuts from him while he carried his brief case and a Kroger grocery bag. They walked inside the building together, grinning as though they admired each other. I left the parking lot after they entered the building. I needed to get a bite to eat because the stake out was about to be on. It was time for Robin Tyler and I to cross paths again. Unfortunately for Robin, the reunion wouldn't be pretty.

Cole

19

*I*t was Friday and Audrie and I had been arguing all week over the phone. She called to check on the children, but they were already at the Clarks' for the weekend. I'd been off work since early in the afternoon because I took a half day—something else for Audrie to fuss about.

"So, you didn't spend any time with them before taking them over there?" she asked, not letting me answer. "Then, why did you take off so early?"

"Are you going to be quiet long enough to let me answer now?"

"Yes, please answer. I've got to hear this."

I sighed. "I didn't want to get caught in the Friday rush hour. The Clarks had plans for the kids this evening, and you know how traffic is on Friday after work. I didn't want to chance ruining their plans."

"Mm-hmm," she said.

"Well, what the hell do you think I took a half-day off for, Audrie?"

"Why are you raising your voice and cussing at me?"

"I'm just tired of arguing. This is silly. We have bigger fish to fry—"

"And speaking of bigger fish: Any word on her whereabouts?"

"Believe me, Audrie, when I get word on Karma's whereabouts, you will be the first person I call. The police have been hanging close by all week, and there has been no sign of her."

"Well, I'm getting off the phone with you now. You said you would be sensitive to how I feel, not wanting to make the same mistake you did with Glenda, but I don't see a change in you at all."

That pissed me off. "Really? Really, Audrie? Well, how about this change." I hung the phone up so hard, I could've broken it.

When the phone rang back, I was sorry that it wasn't broken. I didn't answer it at first. It stopped ringing, and then started again, so I answered.

"Yeah," I said into the phone.

"Cole! I know you didn't hang up on me."

"Have a nice weekend, Audrie. I'll talk to you tomorrow. I have nothing else to say to you."

"Well, bye!"

This time, she hung up. I went over to the bar to fix me a drink. How dare she accuse me of being insensitive. What about how she treated me? I was going through, too, but she didn't seem to give a damn about my feelings.

As I stirred my cranberry and vodka, I noticed the VIP invitation to The Sable Foxx. Robin hadn't been to work in a few days. Her sister called in for her, stating she had a family emergency. I tried to call her the next day, but she didn't answer her phone. I could always go just to see if she would be there, I thought. More thoughts came to mind—that sexy ass strut she had in those heels, the cowgirl costume, her small waist, luscious-looking ass, and the long weave that flowed down her back. That woman was hypnotic. Yes, I wanted to see her in full effect again.

I wasn't worried that anything physical would happen between Robin and me. We would be inside the club, and although I was very angry with Audrie, I had no desire to cheat on her. I looked at the clock and noticed it was nearing the eight o'clock hour. I went to shower and get ready.

I made it to the club about nine-thirty. Once at the front booth, the woman glanced at my VIP invitation and smiled.

"You have a VIP session, sir, and someone is expecting you," she stated.

"Really?" I didn't know what else to say.

"Yes. You know who?"

I wanted to ask if it was Robin, but I didn't remember her stage name. "I think I know," I told her.

The woman smiled again. "Capri, is definitely looking forward to seeing you."

Capri, I thought. *That's it.* I became nervous. She *was* there. "So, what exactly goes on in the VIP sessions?"

"Oh, it's all great fun. Pretty much the same as what goes on out here: Dancing, drinking, small talk and such, except only your eyes get to soak up the show the dancer puts on for you."

I nodded. She fastened my wristband then asked the hostess to lead me to a room. Once inside the room, I took a seat and the girl asked for my drink order. I ordered more vodka since that's what I had before leaving home.

The room was tiny and dimly lit, but darker than inside the main club area. The walls appeared to be white or maybe gray, but the sofa was definitely white. I looked for signs of someone having sex on it before I took a seat. There were none. I thought surely if sex happened in the small rooms, someone would be able to tell, considering the snow white furnishings. It would be too expensive to have the couches cleaned daily. Just as I took a seat, the girl was back with my drink.

"Here you go, Mr. Patterson," she said.

"Thank you," I responded taking the drink then setting it on the table in front of me. "Hey, may I ask you something?"

"Sure," she said.

"Does anything extra go on in these rooms, if you get my drift?"

She shook her head. "No, sir. The girls aren't allowed. The owner doesn't play that. He doesn't want to run the risk of getting shut down. There is at least one security on the outside of each door, and if they even think that's going on in here, they're coming in."

"Oh, okay," I said, nodding.

"But . . . if that's what you're looking for, you might want to ask the girl that comes in here if she'll meet you somewhere away from the club. I know many of the ladies are looking to make some extra dollars, if you get my drift."

I nodded. "Thanks."

"You're welcomed. A Foxx will be in here shortly. Enjoy your drink."

I did just that—enjoyed my drink while taking notice of what all went on in the main area via the flat screen on the wall. My drink was a little strong, but I toughed it out. I was nearly finished and totally smashed when Capri walked in. I tried to straighten up, but I couldn't mask being wasted. My eyes were more than likely tiny slits as I struggled to open them more.

"Hey," I said. "Sorry for my appearance." I tried to speak without slurring, but even I could hear the distorted enunciation of my words. "I didn't mean to get drunk. My drink was a little strong—"

"Sssshhh," she said softly with her finger to her lips.

She picked up the remote then turned the TV to a station that held a list of music. She highlighted Kelly Rowland's "Motivation" and pressed a button to play it.

As the introduction of the song began, she slid the table to the wall and began a slow grind in front of me. Damn, she was fine! She still had the long, dark hair. She wore a pink feathered eye mask along with a baby pink mini-dress. It had a neckline that plunged to her navel. The dress stopped just beneath her butt-cheeks, and as she swayed, I could see a matching thong underneath. She was hot, and she made me hot—in a forbidden way. I was starting to think that maybe it was a bad idea to be there after all. But, my eyes were fixed on her. I couldn't move.

She inched toward me as she danced, pushing each strap from her shoulders. Her breasts were full, youthful and beautiful, but that wasn't the icing. She dropped the dress, revealing her tantalizing, bare body then straddled me. She smelled wonderful. Her perfume was intoxicating. She took my hands and cupped them under her ass as she rotated with sensual grinds, wearing nothing but her pink thong.

I wanted to explode. Hell, I wanted to explode inside of her. Just as I was about to tell her no more, she stood, digging her silver, stiletto heels into the couch and hovered me. She slid her thong aside, exposing her clit and lips with just a small triangle patch of hair, neatly trimmed on top. She began to grind in my face. Now, I knew I couldn't take any more.

When I attempted to get up, she pushed me back down then climbed off the couch. This wasn't right. Robin worked for me. I shouldn't have been there, knowing she and I had to see each other on the job. I was ready to leave. She bent over in front of me, mooning me with the most perfect, caramel-glowing ass. She ripped off her thong, tossing it to the floor then spread her legs some more so I could watch her slide her manicured fingers from one hole to the other. Her fingers began to glisten, and I became so hard at the sight of this woman that I had to put my hand between my legs to ease the throbbing.

She turned and saw me squeezing my midsection. I tried to sit up, so I could brace myself to stand up and leave. That's when I discovered my body felt heavy. My feet and legs felt as though they weighed one hundred pounds each. I thought back to the drink. Was it laced with something? I wondered. How could one drink smash me so hard?

She stepped to me then removed my hand from my midsection. "What are you doing?" I asked.

She didn't respond. Instead, she proceeded to unfasten my pants.

"Hey," I said, trying to lift my arm. I tried to push her off me, but my arm seemed to have no strength. It, too, felt like it weighed a hundred pounds. "Hey, don't do that."

She ignored my demands, and before I could protest any further, she held my erection in one hand and my balls in the other. The warmth and wetness of her mouth sent me into waves of pleasure. This was wrong—so very wrong. They told me this didn't happen—this wouldn't happen—but it was, and it felt so damned good. I tried to control my moans before the security officer on the other side of the door heard me, but this woman was great.

I managed to lift my left hand, but it wasn't to stop her anymore. This time, it was to stroke her head because I was about to cum. I warned her, but she didn't budge. In fact, she sucked me harder as though she wanted it. And I gave it to her. The song went off, and the room was totally quiet. I had landed from cloud nine, and now I felt like shit. She still held me in her hand. I lifted my head to look at her. She continued to kneel between my legs, looking at all I'd released over her face and hands. I peeled off her eye mask, and I nearly screamed like a bitch.

"See, baby. I told you I would swallow you whole again soon," Karma said.

Adrenaline must've been the kick I needed because I jumped up with very little effort this time. I was weak though. I stumbled a bit, but I caught myself.

"Wait a minute, baby," she said, standing before me, stark naked. "I just want us to be a family, Cole. Let's just be a family with our new baby and Shawna and Gavin."

"Get away from me, Karma!"

"Ssshhh . . . please." She glanced at the door. "Let me just talk to you for a minute. I'm sorry I put that stuff in your drink, but I had to be sure you would let me have you tonight."

"What did you do to me?" I asked, leaning against the wall for strength.

"Don't worry, baby. You know I wouldn't hurt you. It'll wear off by morning. I swear."

"What the fuck did you do to me?" I yelled, holding on to my pants. I slid to the floor. Too weak to stand any longer.

"Cole, stop it. Baby, I love you," she said, kneeling on the floor with me.

The door swung open and a couple of security men stormed in. Karma jumped up and darted around them.

"Hey, man, are you alright?" I heard one of them ask.

I couldn't open my eyes. "Call me an ambulance."

Karma

20

---

*A*lthough I told Cole I didn't do anything that would kill him, he passed out and caused a scene. I escaped the club and sat in my car down the street, watching as EMTs loaded Cole onto an ambulance. All I did was sneaked behind the bar and added a little something to his drink. It was some crushed Cialis, so his dick would stay hard and one of Bunny's prescribed sleeping pills. I told the bartender that I'd dealt with Cole before, and that he liked his drink strong. I watched the bartender add more vodka to the cranberry mix and drugs then stir it. His back was turned when I laced the drink, so he had no idea I only told him to make the drink stronger, so Cole wouldn't taste the drugs.

It was a good thing I had a change of clothes in my trunk. I never thought I'd have to hall ass out of the club, butt-naked like that. I followed the ambulance at a distance. I needed to know what hospital my man would be taken to. Once the ambulance pulled around to the emergency room entrance, a nurse ran out, appearing to check Cole's vitals. He wasn't moving. My heart sank. *He should be alright*, I thought. *Or, is he? Did I do too much with com-*

bining the drugs? I panicked. I wanted to rush to Cole's side. Another nurse rushed out with an IV bag hooked to a bed. The EMTs lifted Cole off the gurney and placed him onto the bed. The two nurses hurriedly pushed the bed inside and the automatic doors closed behind them.

I wanted to cry. I didn't mean to hurt Cole. I needed to see him. I needed to know that he would be alright. I pulled into the visitor's parking lot then sat, contemplating a way to get in and see Cole.

Big Mike began blowing up my phone. I ignored him each time I saw his number. He didn't leave messages, so I couldn't tell if he was calling to cuss me out, or to just ask what happened. Either way, I wasn't ready to talk to him.

I took off my dancing wig, and then put on my auburn bob. I went inside the emergency room and walked to the admissions desk.

"Good evening," I said to the salt-and-pepper haired lady. "My husband was just brought here by the ambulance, and I'm trying to find out if he is okay."

"What's your husband's name?"

"Colby Patterson," I answered.

"Just a minute," she said. "I'll be right back."

The woman was only gone a couple of minutes before she came back. "The doctors are still examining him, Mrs. Patterson. Feel free to take a seat, and once it's clear, I'll call you to go back to join your husband. I'll need some ID though."

"So, can you tell me anything? Is he alert and talking?"

"I don't think so ma'am. He didn't appear to be alert when I went back there. But, if you'll hold on just a minute, I'll be sure to get you back in the room with him. Take a seat. I may be calling you back up for some questions about his insurance and such."

I couldn't stick around. Big Mike or Audrie or anyone who could recognize me might show up. I glanced at the entry to the back of the hospital where the patients were. There was a guard at the door, and no one could enter without an entry code. I walked slowly to the waiting area, trying to figure out my next move.

I took a seat next to an old woman who eyed me strangely. "Good evening," I spoke.

She didn't respond—only stared with wide eyes.

"Are you okay?" I asked the woman.

"Yeah," she said matter-of-factly. "What about you?"

"I'm well. I'm just here, waiting to see my husband."

"And who is your husband?" Her eyes were narrowed, and she folded her arms.

I almost didn't answer her, but I figured since she didn't know me, I could say. "Colby Patterson. The ambulance just brought him in. I hope he's okay," I said, fidgeting in my seat.

"Colby Patterson's your husband?" she asked, sounding shocked.

I glanced at her. Her face matched the surprised tone in her voice. "Yes," I answered, frowning.

I didn't know what was up with this old woman, but I figured I better stop talking to her. She definitely seemed to know Cole. I turned away from her then looked over where the guard stood. He held the door open for a couple of patients as they exited. One of them was on a walker and had her purse on her arm. The next time she lifted her walker, her purse fell to the ground. The guard picked it up then offered to walk her out. She smiled and agreed. After they were outside, I knew I needed to make a move.

As I stood, the old woman said, "Don't I know you?"

I turned to her. "No, ma'am. I don't think—"

I stopped because I realized I did know her. She was the old nosy neighbor who lived across the street in Cole's former neighborhood. I finished my thought.

"I don't know you." I kept walking.

"Oh, yes, you do," she yelled.

I moved quickly. I looked back, and the old woman was sliding to the edge of her seat as though she was about to get up. When I turned around, another patient was exiting from the back, so I stole the opportunity to get through the doors.

I was already out of breath, but I couldn't leave there without knowing whether Cole was alright. As I scrambled through the halls, I came upon another work station. Two nurses sat, looking up at me.

"Excuse me," I said, panting. "My husband is back here, and I really need you to help me find him."

"What's his name?" one of them asked.

"Colby Patterson," I responded.

I stretched my neck, trying to see if anyone was coming down the hall for me. The woman typed on her computer keyboard then paused.

"He's here, but we can't let you back right now," she answered.

"Why not? Is he going to be okay? Can't you tell me anything?" I yelled.

Another nurse walked up. "What's going on? What's the problem?" she asked.

The first nurse turned to her. "This is Mr. Patterson's wife. She wants to know how he's doing."

"Oh, I just left him, Mrs. Patterson. He's going to be fine," the other nurse said. "We can't let you in there with him though—not until the doctor is done. The doctor will probably want to speak with you anyway." She reached for my arm. "Let me show you to our waiting area, and I promise I will come get you when you can join him."

I nodded. I could breathe easier now. I'd heard what I wanted to hear—that he would be fine. I walked along side of the woman as she continued to talk. I didn't say anything—just nodded. As we made it to the doors where I sneaked in, two officers came storming through. They charged in so fast, they startled both me and the nurse, sending us against the wall. They never looked at either of us as they forced their way ahead. I needed to get my ass out of there—quick.

"Thank you so much for your help," I said, shaking the woman's hand. "I'll be right out here if you need me."

"Okay, Mrs. Patterson," she answered.

I was through the doors when I heard her respond. The guard I'd seen earlier was just reentering the emergency room as I whizzed by him. He didn't chase me. He just stood in place as though he didn't have a clue why I was in such a hurry. I picked up my pace, looking over my shoulder, and then before I knew it, I was on the ground. I hit the ground hard and hurt my wrist. A wooden cane was pointed in my face, and so I knew what happened. I had been tripped. As I rose to my knees to inspect my injury, I looked up at the old woman from the past as she stood over me.

"I knew it was you!" she yelled. "You're a monster. You killed Mrs. Patterson!" She raised her cane over her head. "How dare you do that to such a nice woman!"

WHAM, WHAM

She delivered two hard blows to my back. That cane felt like it was made of cement instead of wood. I had to come to my feet in a hurry. As the next blow came down, I caught it. The contact stung the palm of my hand, but at least my fingers were spared. I snatched the cane, causing the old woman to lose her balance. She fell just as hard as I had. I lifted the cane to show her what it felt like, but the security officer yelled and ran toward me.

"Hey! Hey! Stop that! Get away from her!"

I dropped the cane then ran toward my car. I clicked the lock on my remote and hopped in the car almost in one sweeping action. My hands shook as I started the car. I pulled out of the space then drove full speed ahead toward the old woman as the security officer tried to help her up. He looked up and saw me coming. His eyes looked as if he'd seen a ghost. He was definitely scared, but I was determined. I pressed the gas pedal harder. Just as I was about to make contact with them, the officer found strength to drag himself and the old woman in the clear. I missed them. *Damn!* I thought.

There was no time to go back. I needed to get away from there. I balled out of the hospital parking lot like lightening—fast.

Cole

21

I was awakened in the hospital by an attractive mocha-colored nurse as she checked my vitals. I glanced around the room, wondering how I'd gotten there. A monitor repeatedly beeped next to my bed. The noise was irritating, and I wondered why the nurse acted as if she didn't hear it. She released my wrist then wrote something on a clipboard after looking at her watch. She glanced at me and seemed surprised to see my eyes opened.

"Oh, Mr. Patterson, you're awake."

I swallowed then tried to speak. "Am . . . am I really in the hospital?"

"Yes, sir, you are. How do you feel?"

I stared at her for a moment before answering. My mind was a bit foggy. Why had she asked me this? Should I feel okay? I wondered. "I'm okay, I think." The beeping continued. The sound was piercing each time it went off. "What is that beeping? Can you do something about it?"

"Sure. I was just about to do that. It's time for another IV bag. I have one right here."

I watched as she pressed some buttons on the machine then replaced the empty IV bag.

"Great. I'll get the doctor to come see you, and then if you want breakfast, I'll have some brought to you."

Cartoons were on the flat screen TV that hung from the ceiling in the corner. Then, a commercial came on, suggesting more cartoons were next. The nurse turned to leave.

"I'll be back shortly, Mr. Patterson."

"Um, ma'am," I called.

"Yes, Mr. Patterson," she answered, heading back toward me.

"Is today Saturday?" I asked, glancing at the TV.

She smiled. "Oh, yes, it's Saturday. I know it may seem like it, but you really weren't out for that long, Mr. Patterson."

"So, I just came here last night?"

"Right. You were passed out when you came in, but you're in good condition now. Let me go get the doctor. He'll be able to tell you more."

When she left the room, I lay there thinking, trying to remember all that happened the night before. It was Saturday. Where was Audrie? I wondered. Then, in a flash, it came to me. *Audrie left earlier in the week. She went to Dallas to see her mom. So, yesterday was Friday. I talked to Audrie, but we argued. We argued, and she'd pissed me off.* It was all coming back now. I continued to piece things together in my mind.

I went out . . . to the club—The Sable Foxx. Robin! I wanted to see Robin. Wait? Did I see her?

The doctor entered the room, and the same nurse was right behind him. He was a slender, older white man. He stepped to the side of my bed and spoke.

"Mr. Patterson, how are you?" he said. "I'm Dr. Bailey."

"I'm okay, Dr. Bailey. I'd like to know what's going on with me though."

"Sure. I hear you're having a little trouble remembering some things, so I'll do my best to help you."

"Great," I responded.

"Well, I hear you've already learned that today is Saturday, and that you came to the emergency room last night."

"Right," I said.

"Do you recall going to a club and being entertained by one of the dancers?"

My mind began to race. I remembered being in one of the VIP rooms, and then a flash of the pink mini-dress came to mind. Then, I remembered her removing the pink feathered mask. *Karma!*

"Yes! It was Karma," I said.

"Pardon me?" the doctor asked.

"Karma Jolley . . . the escapee from the mental institution—"

"Oh, yes," Dr. Bailey said. "That's what the police say they need to talk to you about. A detective from the fugitive department gave us his card and said he wanted to speak with you when you were able."

I tried to sit up, but the nurse placed her hand on my shoulder to motion me back down.

"Please . . . I've got to get out of here," I said. "This woman is crazy. Are there police in the hospital?"

"Yes," Dr. Bailey answered. "As a matter of fact, there are two right outside your door."

"The police were called to the club along with the ambulance. Once the police learned who you were, they were familiar with your case. They've been here since you were admitted."

"So, what did she do to me?"

"It seems your drink was fixed with an erectile dysfunction drug and a sleeping pill."

"A sleeping pill? Is that why I slept so long and can hardly remember anything today?"

"Yes. The woman in question wasn't very careful about the doses of the medications."

"Wait a minute. There are police on the other side of the door? That means she got away, didn't she?"

"I'm not sure," he answered. "Perhaps that's something the detectives can answer for you."

"She could have killed me!" I fussed.

"Well, I wouldn't say she put that much in your drink, but the substances were quite a bit. But don't worry. We've cleaned your system, and you should be fine when we send you home later today."

"I wish I could go back to sleep then wake up and realize this was all a nightmare."

"I can only imagine," the doctor said. "Oh, by the way . . . we weren't certain if there was someone you wanted us to call, so we—"

"Please do *not* tell me you contacted my wife."

"Well, the police gathered your cell phone and other items and noticed a number listed as *sweetie*—"

I tried to sit, but was again pressed to the bed by the nurse. "Oh, no . . . oh, no . . . you didn't! Please tell me you didn't call my wife."

"We didn't call her," he said. I let out a loud sigh. "I wanted to wait until you were alert."

"Thank you! Thank you! I'm so glad you didn't call her. I'll call on my own. Where is my phone?"

The nurse walked over to the stand beside the bed then slid the drawer open. "All of your things are here, Mr. Patterson."

"Great. Thank you. Thank you so much."

The doctor gave me orders for rest when I got home and suggested I call my wife to be by my side as soon as possible. That was easy for him to say, considering he wasn't the one who would have to explain the reason for being in the strip club in the first place. Audrie was already mad at me for keeping the secret of the roses sent by Karma. This new incident that landed me in the hospital would probably put our marriage in serious trouble. Still, I needed to tell her. I knew that if I didn't, Karma certainly would.

Karma

22

I sat in my hotel room, watching Cole, on the TV, exiting the hospital with a swarm of news reporters around him. He seemed annoyed, but he answered as many of their questions about what happened at the club as he could without blowing up at them. There seemed to be ten or more microphones extended over his head, and the cameras followed as he walked toward a Yellow Cab. He stopped and turned to them just after reaching the cab.

"Listen," he said. "Please do not follow me to my home. I have children, and I don't want them traumatized by all of you in front of our home."

"Will you just answer a couple of more questions, Mr. Patterson," a feminine voice asked. "Is it true you once had an affair with the escapee, and now there is question of paternity regarding a baby recently born by her?"

The blood seemed to drain from his face. "An affair?" he said. "There was no affair. My wife and I are happy and solely dedicated to each other—always have been since we met."

"Liar!" I screamed at the TV.

How dare he deny his love for me! He made love to me, and he knew it. I sat up, fuming as the scene continued.

"So, then you contest there is a possibility you could be the father of her newborn?"

He opened the door to the cab. "Absolutely none. Karma Jolley is conniving and sex-crazed. Anyone who would even believe the words of this irrational, mentally-challenged woman must surely have a psychological problem, also."

He jumped into the cab, reminding them all to stay away from his house. I turned off the TV then began to pace. All the media seemed to be about me and what happened with Cole at the club. Nobody was looking for the Robin-chick, or so it seemed. I'd watched the news all week, but nothing came up about her.

I lay in wait for Robin to exit from her job that evening. She got into her car then pulled off. I was right behind her, but she was clueless. She wasn't much of a defensive driver at all because I never once saw her glance into her rearview mirror to see what was behind her. She made my job easy.

I parked only two spaces over from her once she pulled into a department store parking lot at the Oakcourt Mall. She got out of her car then headed into the department store. Though the sun was getting low, I slid on my sunglasses then trailed her, allowing her to get several steps ahead of me. I had my eye on her. I had no intentions of losing sight of her.

Once in the department store, I watched her pick up a few blouses, a skirt, and a pair of slacks. She went inside the dressing room area. I walked slowly toward the room, surveying the area. Robin was the only one in the dressing room, and the sales associate was on the other side of the women's department, straightening clothes. I looked back at the associate, but she was too busy. She didn't see me enter the dressing room.

When I walked in, Robin had just exited her space, wearing only her bra and the skirt she picked up. She walked toward the long mirror on the wall between the enclosed dressing spaces. She obviously didn't recognize me with my shades on because she spoke and continued to admire herself in the mirror. I pretended to like her choice.

"Oh, that's beautiful on you," I said.

"Thank you," she said, straightening the skirt. "I wanted to try it in black, but I was thinking I have so much black already."

"Oh, no, that mustard looks great on you. What type of blouse would you wear with it?"

She turned without looking in my face then walked toward her dressing space. "I picked one off the rack that might work. It's in here."

When she walked inside the enclosed space, I took the liberty to shove her completely inside then stepped in with her and locked the door. She was startled.

"Hey!" she yelled.

I silenced her quickly with one blow of her head into the dressing room wall. The thud was so hard, the entire space shook. She slid to the floor, her eyes closed and head bleeding. The associate entered, calling out to Robin.

"Hello? Ma'am? Are you okay?" she asked.

"Yes, I'm fine," I answered. "Sorry about the noise. I bumped the wall by mistake. I'm okay though."

The woman hesitated then said. "Oh . . . well . . . okay. Are you sure you're alright? You seemed to have hit the wall pretty hard."

I wanted to say, "Bitch, didn't I say I was fine!" But I refrained. Instead, I held my composure then spoke in a polite tone. "Oh, yes, I fine. The wall is okay, too," I joked.

She laughed. "Okay. Well, let me know if you need me for anything. I'll be straightening racks just across from this area."

"Okay," I said.

When I heard the bell chime, signaling she'd left the dressing area, I checked Robin's breathing. She wasn't breathing, and I couldn't seem to find a pulse. I grabbed her purse then eased out of the dressing room. The associate was in the very spot she said she'd be, so I ducked behind clothing racks until I'd cleared the store and was on my way out of the mall.

I combed the news all week, looking for information about Robin, but I saw nothing. I called into her job though, saying I was Robin's sister, and that she would not be in the rest of the week due to a family emergency. The woman I spoke to promised to get the information to Cole.

I must've paced for thirty minutes after seeing that news report. I needed a fool-proof plan to get Cole to accept me and our baby into his life. He wasn't going to listen to anything I had to say with Audrie in the picture, so first things first—I was going to have to get rid of Audrie.

My family and I were going to need a cushion of cash to survive on after I killed Audrie, and we went on the run. Cole probably had some money saved up, but I wanted to show him that I could contribute, too. Then, it hit me. Tremaine was my ticket, and he still owed me big time. I grabbed my cell off the bed then dialed his number. I took a chance on the fact that he might not have seen the news.

"What's up," he said softly into the phone.

"I need to see you," I said. "It's important."

"Say what?"

"You heard me. I need for you to meet me with five thousand dollars."

"What the—" he started but cut himself off. "For what?"

"Does it really matter? You're going to get that much in services from me."

He whispered, "And what's that? What you got in mind?"

"A good time . . . believe me. You won't be sorry."

He spoke up a little. "Look, you gon' havta be more specific, if you want to get five Gs out of me."

"Nigga, please. You know what I'm working with, and you also know that you've underpaid me. Now quit acting like you don't want it, and meet me at my hotel room."

"Not right now, shawty. I still got issues at home. We gon' havta chill for a minute."

"Bullshit! You've had more than enough chill time. You need to get your ass to my hotel room in half an hour."

He huffed. "Who the fuck you think you're talking to? I don't know who you're used to—"

"I know who I'm talking to, and I said have your ass at my hotel in half an hour or forget you knew me."

He paused so long, it was hard to tell he was still on the phone. He was there though. As I listened closer, I could hear his TV in the background. I panicked, wondering if he had been watching the news. If he'd seen my picture on TV, my cover was blown and the opportunity to hatch my plan would never come. I couldn't take more of the silence.

"So, what's it going to be?" I asked him. "I thought you liked this pussy."

"All I'm saying is I need more time," he finally said, whispering. "Wifey is all up in my grill since catching you over here. I don't know when I can sneak out."

I wasn't expecting this, but what could I do? I would have to hold out, but not for long. If the news continued to replay Cole's story and show my mug shot and hospital picture, someone was bound to recognize me. I didn't want to stay hemmed up in my room for days. Besides, how would I get food? I decided to give Tremaine an ultimatum.

"Look. I have others lined up, waiting to take care of me. You said you wanted me exclusively, but I've got bills and other needs to be met. If you can't be the one and only to take care of me when I need it, then I'm going to throw away this phone you gave me and start sharing my goods."

"Hey, shawty, you trippin'," he said.

"I'm only going to hold out for one more day, Tremaine. You need to find a way to see me tomorrow by noon."

"A'ight. I can do that," he answered, his voice more elevated now. It was apparent his wife walked into the room. "Yeah, man. We can make that happen."

"Good," I said, smiling. "See you tomorrow."

"That's what's up. A'ight. Peace."

He hung up, and I couldn't be happier. Tremaine had no idea what was in store for him the next day. He was about to become more familiar with my hotel bed than he could've ever imagined.

Cole

23

---

*O*n Sunday, I called Audrie home. She wanted to know why, but I couldn't tell her over the phone. I hadn't even contemplated how I would deliver the news. This was going to be hard. Not only had I gone back to The Sable Foxx where I thought my assistant, Robin, worked, but I was in a VIP room, thinking I was getting oral favor by her—only it was Karma. My worst enemy didn't even deserve to be in my shoes.

That damned Karma was crazy, but clever. I didn't know a soul who schemed the way she did. Never once had I seen a resemblance between Karma and Robin. Robin was slightly thicker, but then again, I hadn't seen Karma after she had her baby. And the hair—how could I see that coming? Karma's hair was short the last time I saw them haul her off to do her sentence. She either wore a weave or a wig at the club. I should've known the only way she could stay off the police's radar was to change her appearance. Still, how in the hell would I explain all of this to my wife?

Audrie's flight was scheduled to land in Memphis by ten A.M. I sent a car service to pick her up, fearing she'd want to discuss why I'd called her back from her visit with her mom. I figured it would be better if she was in the comforts of our home before I broke the news to her.

I started breakfast once she called to say the driver was only ten minutes from our house. I thought perhaps she'd be hungry, but I have to admit I knew the breakfast would be a stalling tool. I wished somehow there was a way around letting her know, but there wasn't. My one-night hospital stay was all over the news, so I had no doubt that Audrie would hear about it one way or another.

She entered the house, calling for me. "Cole! I'm home. Where are you?"

"In the kitchen," I yelled to her.

She stepped into the kitchen, eyeing me suspiciously. "What's going on?" she asked. "Why the car service?"

I walked over to her then kissed her lips. "Hey, sweetie. I figured I'd just stay here and have breakfast ready for you. That's all," I lied. "How was your flight?"

"My flight was fine. Now, really . . .what's going on?"

"Huh?" I said, not ready to give her any information. I turned toward the stove. "Oh, sweetie, I hope you're hungry because I've cooked all of this for you."

I made hash browns, eggs, bacon, canned biscuits, and cut up some orange slices and strawberries. Audrie liked coffee and water with her breakfast. A fresh pot of coffee brewed while I cooked. After turning over the bacon, I fixed a glass of ice water, and then set it on the table in front of Audrie. She had taken a seat, apparently awaiting an explanation.

Once all the food was done, I fixed Audrie's plate then set it in front of her. "Eat up, sweetie. I know it's been a while, but I just wanted to show you that your husband can still cook—breakfast, that is." I smiled, but Audrie didn't return one.

Now that I didn't have anything to do, I became nervous. I excused myself from the kitchen, telling Audrie I'd be back once I thought she had finished eating. I went into our bedroom and plopped on the bed. *Why didn't I just stay home?* I thought. I had no business going back to that club. *I've just got to tell her and get it over with.*

I went back into the kitchen and took a seat across from Audrie. She still had plenty of food on her plate. As I watched her, I understood why. She chewed each bite nearly a hundred times before she swallowed. She was clearly bothered by the thought of what I might tell her. She'd been hurt so much already, and it was killing me to have to give her more news that would tear at her heart. I took a deep breath then began.

"Sweetie, hear me out, okay?"

She nodded then set down her fork. "I'm listening."

"We've been arguing a lot lately . . . over something that is beyond both of our control, and it took a toll on me. I didn't know how to handle it." I paused. That part was easy, but beginning the rest was hard. "I . . . I, um . . . I—"

"Cole, get it out already! I know it can't be good news since I had to come home, so just come on with it."

Beads of perspiration lined my forehead, and I knew Audrie could see them. I tried to play it off though. "Wow, it's hard work, cooking in this kitchen," I said, wiping my forehead. "I don't know how you do it." She just looked at me. "How's your breakfast, sweetie?"

"Cold," she snapped. "And I'm done, so talk." She slid her plate to the middle of the table.

That stall didn't last long at all. I needed to continue, but just that quick, I made up my mind that I wouldn't tell her everything. I wanted to spare her some of the pain, if I could.

"Audrie, I was pissed at you, so I went back to The Sable Foxx for drinks," I started.

"And?" she asked with raised eyebrows.

"And you'll never believe who I ran into."

"Robin!" she yelled. "You already told me you saw her there the last time you went in that sinful place. Why did you go back?"

"The club sent me a free pass, and I told you: I was pissed at you. I just wanted to have some drinks and clear my head," I lied.

"This can't be all. I know you called me home for more, Cole, so out with it."

I cleared my throat. "It wasn't Robin I ran into, Audrie. It was Karma."

Her eyes widened. "What! You saw her?"

"Yes, and we had a huge altercation and—"

"You actually saw and spoke to her?"

159

"Sweetie, I know I doubted you before, but please forgive me. We have extra security now, and the authorities are looking for her more aggressively since Friday."

"What the hell was she doing in the strip club—" she started then cut herself off. She picked up her plate then walked over to the microwave. "Never mind. I'm sure she followed you there—just like she followed me to the grocery store." Audrie placed her plate in the microwave then set the timer.

"Sweetie—"

"Well, at least now everybody knows I'm not crazy. Even my mom thought I was losing my mind."

"But, sweetie—"

"And now that I'm home, I'm not running from her ass anymore. I've had enough time to do some thinking. People like Karma don't just go away. They have to be gotten rid of."

The microwave chimed. Audrie opened it and removed her plate. She headed back to the table and took her seat.

"So, what are you saying, Audrie? You want a gun?"

"Yeah," she answered, sticking a forkful of eggs in her mouth.

"You don't know how to shoot a gun."

"That's why they have shooting ranges—for people like me who want to learn. We should go together."

I wasn't sure I should say any more at this point. The next thing would be to keep her from watching the news for a couple of days. By then, the story would probably die down.

Audrie ate at a normal pace now. She seemed a little relieved even. I refused to disturb that peace. I stood then turned to leave.

"I think that's a great idea, sweetie. We can go to the range together on the weekend."

"Sounds great," she answered just before taking a bite of her biscuit.

"I'm going to take a shower. I have smoke in my hair, and I'm a bit sweaty."

She nodded and waved her hand. It was true that I could smell the aroma of the food on my body, and I was sweaty. But, my sweat glands were overactive because I knew I hadn't told Audrie everything. I went to our bedroom and jumped in the shower in our master bath. I was no less stressed than I was before Audrie had come home. The thought of Karma actually stalking me and my family again was devastating.

Audrie was right. We needed to protect ourselves at all costs. Karma had killed before, and she would more than likely kill again. I had a notion that perhaps I should take some time off work while Audrie was on leave, so we could take shooting lessons sooner. I never wanted to learn to fire a weapon, but dealing with Karma made me rethink that. I turned off the water then stepped out of the shower and grabbed a towel. I finished drying off then went into our bedroom to find something to put on. I didn't get the chance because Audrie's scream pierced through the closed bedroom door.

I charged out of the bedroom and into the kitchen, thinking I'd face an intruder. No one was there except Audrie. She sat at the table, wailing with a flow of tears down her face. My heart was in my throat, and I was confused.

"What is it, sweetie? Are you okay?"

She shook her head and screamed some more, pulling her hair. I tucked my towel around my waist then walked over and grabbed her hands. She struggled free.

"Let me go! Let me go," she cried.

"Audrie, what's wrong? What's going on with you?"

She picked up her cell, pressed a few buttons then tossed it at me. I caught it then took a look at the mini-motion picture that played before me. My heart plunged from my throat to my stomach. Audrie had every right to scream, and now, I wished I could, too, as I watched a clear video of Karma giving me oral sex in the club.

Karma

24

I sat, wondering if Audrie enjoyed my show. She needed to know how much of a pro I am at giving oral pleasure to the man she married. The video certainly displayed how much he loved being on the receiving end of my favors. I got her cell number from one of her coworkers. I contacted her office on Friday, pretending to be Robin from the other location. I told them I had an emergency, and I couldn't reach my boss, Cole, on his cell. They offered me Audrie's cell number with no fuss.

When Cole's eyes were closed, I pulled out my cell and held my arm out in an angle that would capture us in action. Audrie had to have loved the wink I gave her near the end with her husband's penis pressed against my lips. The footage was too perfect, and I knew that if Audrie didn't leave after that, nothing would make her leave. I was only trying to spare Cole's heart. He took Glenda's death rather hard, so I hoped to aggravate Audrie enough to make her go on her own. I was damned near out of patience though.

It was one o'clock in the afternoon, and Tremaine was an hour late for our tryst. He promised to meet me at my room by noon. I looked under my bed for the items I would need once he arrived. They were all in place. I smiled, knowing today was going to be a good day. That was Ice Cube who'd said that in a song once. This day would be good alright. In fact, it would be great, given I would force Tremaine to help me carry out my plans with his money.

Knock, knock, knock.

He was at the door. It had to be him because no one else knew where I lived. I straightened my form-fitting dress, which accented every curve of my nude body underneath. I peeped through the hole to make sure it was Tremaine before I opened the door. He was so tall, all I could see was his neck. I started to unlock the door, but then it dawned on me that perhaps he'd seen me on the news already and had the police with him. Now my nerves were shot. I stood behind the door, not knowing what to do. Before I knew it, I asked who was it.

"Yeah?" I said, using a deep masculine voice.

"Um, I must have the wrong door," he said.

"Who you looking for?"

"Capri," he said.

"There's no Capri here," I answered, still using the manly tone.

"Sorry 'bout that, dawg," he said then turned to walk away.

When he stepped from the door and started down the hall, I eased the door open and peeped out at him. He was alone. He pulled his cell out of his pocket as he started toward the elevator. I decided to call him back.

"Psst." He didn't look back. "Psst," I repeated.

That time, he turned around. "What the—"

I placed my finger to my lip then beckoned him with my hand. "C'mon," I whispered.

He walked quickly back to my room. I stepped back to allow him in then locked the door.

"Girl, what's wrong with you?" He frowned.

"Nothing. Why do you ask?"

He looked around the room. "You got company, or something?"

"Naw. Why?" I walked over to the bed then sat down.

"Then what was that all about at the door?"

"Nothing. I'm a woman living here alone, so I just wanted to make sure you weren't one of my perverted neighbors or some dude who followed me from the club last night," I lied with ease.

He shook his head. "You need me to take you from that lifestyle, don't you?" He sat next to me.

"Would you?"

"Only if you promise to give it to me and only me."

"Well, that's not fair. You've got in-house stuff, but you want me to commit to you, too?"

"What's wrong with that? You'll be taken care of."

I shrugged. "I guess I see your point."

"You got something to drink around here?"

I stood. "Absolutely."

I walked over to the refrigerator then made him a similar concoction to the one I made for Cole. I made sure enough fruit juice was in it so that he wouldn't taste the pills. When I looked back at him, he had just gotten up and went to the table to get the remote.

"Shawty, why you staying in a joint like this?"

"Why not? Utilities and cable are included. Besides, it's all I can do for now."

"Yeah, I see I'm gon' havta change that. You with a real one now," he said taking a seat on the couch. "Just keep working that ass like you do for me, and I gotchu." I didn't say anything. "You hear me?"

I turned and started toward him with the drink. "Mm-hmm. I hear you. I gotchu, too." I smiled.

He reached for his drink then took it straight to his lips. "Damn, shawty, if I had wanted slushy, I would've stopped by Sonic on the way."

"Oh, my bad. Too much ice?"

"Too much ice, and too much juice, or whatever the hell that sweet shit is you got in it."

I took the drink from him then headed back toward the kitchen area. I was too glad to add more vodka to the glass. He just didn't know. In ten minutes or less, it was going to be on.

After pouring more vodka into his drink, I went over and handed it to him then sat beside him.

"This is more like it," he said just after taking a sip. "So, what's up, shawty? What made you call me over?"

"I'm in bad shape. I need that money I asked you for."

He took a big gulp of his drink then said. "I brought it, but first, I need to know what you got for me." He leaned over and kissed me. "Damn, I love kissing those soft lips."

"Oh, yeah? Well, I like kissing something else of yours. How about you just finish that drink then climb up on that bed over there."

He licked his lips, looking me up and down. He took another gulp then slurred a little. "We haven't really had a chance to talk since you were last at my place, but I need to apologize for that interruption."

The thought of how the wife I never knew he had came home and wanted to beat my ass made me mad. I smirked. "No, I guess we haven't talked about that, huh?" He sipped his drink. "Let's just talk about that later. Right now I need you to finish that drink."

"Impatient, aren't you, shawty?"

"You have no idea," I answered.

He downed the remaining contents of the glass then stood and began undressing. I headed to the bed then pulled my dress over my head before climbing on top. Tremaine's long, nude frame walked toward the bed, leaning at an angle. Even he knew something was not right with him.

"Damn, I feel like I'm walking on pillows," he said, looking like a human Leaning Tower of Pisa.

He barely made it to the bed before he toppled on his back. His eyes were closed, but I knew he wasn't asleep.

"Are you okay?" I asked.

He slurred even more. "What the fuck is going on?" he asked, seemingly unable to open his eyes.

"You're about to find out real soon," I told him.

I climbed out of the bed then pulled out the rope and other items I purchased to restrain him. When I climbed on top of him, he thought I was about to give him sex, but I only got on top of him to tie him to the bed.

"Can you get it up for me, baby?" he asked.

I looked at his limp noodle then laughed. I didn't crush a Cialis for him as I did for Cole. That was because I had no intention of screwing him. I had other plans for him that didn't involve sex. Once his life would be spared, he'd gladly pay me and thank me later.

Cole

25

*A*udrie pounded on me a while. I held her arms until she calmed down. We were knotted on the floor in the kitchen as she screamed and cried to the top of her lungs.

"Get off me! Pleeeeeaaaassseee, just get off me!" she cried.

"No, sweetie. Not until I know you're okay." I sat with my legs and arms enveloping her.

"Cole, get off me!" Her breathing was labored. She sucked in air slowly then yelled, "If you don't get off me, Cole, I swear to God—"

"Audrie, baby, I love you. Please calm down, so we can talk."

She let out a few more wails before she said anything. "Whyyyyy? Why, Cole? How could you? I don't deserve this!"

"I know, sweetie. It wasn't you. It was me. I was stupid, baby. I'm so sorry."

"Cole, get off me. Pleeeeaaaassseee. Oh, my God, I don't believe this! Just let me go!"

"Are you going to be okay, Audrie?"

"I'm done swinging at you, if that's what you want to know. But I'm NOT okay!"

I released her and hoped for the best. She sat up on her knees then pulled herself up on the table. I got up quickly then reattached my towel to my waist. Audrie stared at me with tear-stained cheeks, shaking her head. She deserved some type of explanation, but I knew nothing I could say would suffice. Still, I had to make an attempt to soothe things over before the children came home.

"Just sit down, sweetie. I'll tell you everything."

She shook her head. "Un-un. I don't trust you. You've played me for crazy all this time, but your ass knew—"

"Audrie, I didn't know anything. If you'll just please sit down, I'm going to tell you what I found out. Sit down, sweetie."

Her face hardened and she frowned as though she spied something disgusting. She glared at me through squinted eyes that released an abundance of tears. I felt low, and I wished I could just go and hide somewhere. But there was no way out of this. I couldn't leave her hanging in her pain, wondering and guessing what might've happened. I had to tell her something. When she parted her lips, her tone was stern.

"I'm going to sit down, Cole, but you better tell me everything."

"I am, sweetie. I promise."

I walked over and pulled out the table chair she sat in before. She slowly sat down, keeping her eyes on me. I pulled my chair close to hers then reached for her hand. She snatched from me.

"Don't touch me, Cole."

"I just want to—"

"Start talking. That's all I want from you right now—to hear words flowing from your mouth."

"Okay." I sat up straight. "Audrie, you know I love you, right?"

"Cole, that's the same bullshit people on Maury Povich or some other talk show say before giving their spouse the bad news. I'm not trying to hear your I-love-you's right now. I just want to hear the truth about you and Karma."

"There is no me and Karma, sweetie."

"Then, don't beat around the bush! Tell me what the hell is going on!"

It was clear she had become more angry than hurt, so I began. Audrie sat silently and listened to everything I had to say. She mainly shook her head as I talked. I didn't know if she believed my half-truths or not, but I rambled anyway. When I finished, she got up from the table then went into the bedroom and threw herself on the bed. I lay on the bed with her, not knowing what else to do or say.

By eight o'clock that night, I left the house to pick up the children. On the ride over there, I decided to ask Glenda's parents why they had chosen to visit her burial site without me. Mrs. Clark opened the door.

"Good evening, Cole," she said.

"Good evening, Mrs. Clark. How are you?"

"Oh, not too bad," she responded.

"Hey, Cole," Mr. Clark said, entering the room.

"Hi, Mr. Clark."

"Have a seat, Cole," Mrs. Clark said. "The kids are getting their things together now. I told them you were probably on your way. They kept watching that Disney movie," she said, pointing at the TV, "so I told them if they weren't ready when you got here, you were going to leave them. They didn't budge, but you should've seen them scrambling to the back when you rang the door bell." She laughed. "I'll go make sure they don't leave anything behind." She turned to leave.

"Oh, Mrs. Clark, hold on a minute, please."

"Yes," she spun around and said.

I looked at Mr. Clark. "May I speak with you, also, Mr. Clark?"

He nodded, and then they eased on the couch beside each other. I sat across from them in the chair.

"I hear you all went to visit Glenda's grave site," I started. They glanced at each other then back at me. "I'm usually a part of that. Has something changed?"

Mrs. Clark cleared her throat to speak, but Mr. Clark patted her hand then took over. "Cole, we did visit the cemetery this weekend, but we didn't exclude you for reasons you may be thinking," he said.

"Well, I didn't think anything in particular. In fact, I don't have a clue what I've done, if anything."

Mr. Clark spoke as delicately as he could. "It's just that many times, you bring along Audrie. We had something special and private planned for the visit this time—

172

for Glenda's birthday—and we only wanted our immediate family there."

Glenda's birthday! I thought. In all of the mess with Karma, I'd let Glenda's birthday slip my mind. I must've looked like a deer caught in headlights because Mrs. Clark attempted to soothe things over.

"Cole, we wanted you there," she said. "We really did, but we didn't know how to ask you to leave Audrie behind. We thought that might hurt her feelings, too. We didn't want to hurt either of you, but we also wanted our privacy. I hope you understand."

I couldn't shake the thought of having missed Glenda's birthday. Mrs. Clark called my name, snapping me out of the daze.

"Oh, yes, ma'am," I answered. "I'm fine. I respect your wishes. I just needed to know if I had done something that upset you all. Thanks for letting me know."

Shawna and Gavin came into the living room, dragging their bags. They each had an extra tote, obviously some things the Clarks purchased for them. I stood then picked up a few of the bags.

"Go, give your grandparents a kiss," I told them.

They did as told. The Clarks watched us leave their driveway. I didn't say much to the children as we drove home. I mainly prayed about my stress-filled life and thought about how different things would be if Glenda were alive.

Once we got home, the children were surprised to see Audrie at home when we returned. Audrie and I had explained that she would be gone for much longer, so when we returned from the Clarks, Shawna and Gavin were quite happy to see her. She embraced them, talked about how their week and weekend had gone, and then tucked them both into bed. I waited for her to get into bed with me, but she only came back to our room to get a pillow.

"Where are you going?" I asked.

"I'm sleeping in the room with Shawna," she said, snatching her pillow off the bed.

I sat up. "Aren't we going to talk about this?"

She stopped just before leaving the room then whipped her neck around at me. "Cole, I think we've done all the talking necessary for one day, don't you think?"

"But did you hear me, Audrie? I never went there with the intention of cheating. I was poisoned. I couldn't help what happened."

"Yeah, I know, Cole. But, what really hurts right now is that you didn't consider my feelings before you went back there. You wanted to see Robin, and so you went."

"Who said I wanted to see Robin?"

"Oh, come on! You knew, or at least thought she worked there. Why in the world would you go back there, knowing your assistant would be there practically naked?"

"Audrie, I don't want any woman but you, if that's what you're thinking."

She smirked. "Yeah, I know. And that's why you were in a funky-ass strip club, taking advantage of a VIP offer sent to you. Yeah, that makes a whole lot of sense to me, Cole."

"Audrie, if I could take it all back, I would."

"Really? Really, Cole? After you've had your dick in Karma's mouth . . . now you would take it back?"

"I told you I couldn't help that!"

She pushed our bedroom door closed—hard. "You sat in a VIP room, waiting to be entertained! Cole, I think you *could* help it! You didn't have to be there!"

I sighed. "Alright. I see your point. I'm sorry, sweetie. I really am."

"Did you get the paternity results back, yet?"

"No. I've already told you it will be a minute before I get that. Why are you asking me about it again?"

"Because!"

"Audrie, lower your voice, and 'because' isn't an answer. Because why?"

"Because I'm sick of this—sick of not knowing, and sick of her thinking she has to have you because of that baby."

"Audrie, she's mentally ill. I can't control what she thinks. That baby isn't mine."

"But what if she is?"

"Don't say that!" Now it was my turn to yell. "She's not!"

"You don't know that, Cole."

I sighed. I was beyond frustrated. "Alright. You're right. I don't know. I also don't know what else to say."

She turned to leave. "Just don't say anything," she said with her back turned. "I've already told you I don't want to talk about this anymore tonight anyway. This is just too much." Her voice trembled.

She opened the door then walked out on me. I plopped on my pillow, frustrated. I didn't mean to hurt her—again. She was right. I made the wrong choice in going to that club again. Yes, I was mad at her, but I should've thought things through.

Karma

26

*M*orning came, bringing some heavy rain with it. As the thunder roared, the windows rattled a bit, but Tremaine was still fast asleep. I waited until the storm passed then went to open the blinds. Tremaine stirred a bit when the outdoor light illuminated his face. The clouds were still gray, so it wasn't very bright, but Tremaine seemed bothered anyway. I watched him desperately try to focus as I stood over him. He was butt-naked, tied to the table chair with his arms behind his back and his ankles to the legs of the chair. His mouth was bound with a thick scarf. He tried to say something, but all I could hear was mumbling. I slid the scarf down slightly to hear what he had to say.

"What the fuck are you doing?" he fussed.

I laughed. "It's payback time."

"Payback? What?"

I slapped him so hard the chair rocked, and I had to grab it quickly to steady it. He narrowed his eyes and breathed hard as he looked at me.

"That hurt, huh?" I smiled. He didn't say anything, but I answered for him. "Yeah, it did. I know it did because my hand is stinging," I said, shaking my hand.

"What's up, Capri? I don't play these types of games. I ain't into fetishes and chains and whips and shit."

I slapped him again—with the back of my left hand. This time he grunted. That stung like hell, too. He slowly turned his face toward me, heaving as though he just ran full court twice during a basketball game.

"Did I ask you what you were into?" I snapped. "You sure as hell didn't give *me* an option," I said, not letting him answer.

"What are you talking about?"

"Your wife, mutherfucker! You had me sleeping at your house, knowing your wife could walk in on us at any time?"

"She came home early. She was supposed to be in Los Angeles, taking a business workshop. My bad, Capri."

"Damn right it's your bad. But, I can't let you get away with it."

"What do you mean? I thought you called me over here to give you some money."

"Oh, I've got that. I collected that while you were knocked out."

"You got my money? You owe me for that."

That was funny as hell. I laughed so hard, I had to lean on the dresser for support.

"I gave you your money's worth last night," I said between laughing and catching my breath. "Sorry you don't remember it."

"Aw, hell naw, Capri. You can't be for real."

I nodded. "I'm so for real. Maybe I should've recorded it somehow so you'd have some memories."

"Damn. What did you do to me? How come I don't remember?"

"Don't worry. I'll take care of you a little later, too. I've got somewhere to go right now though."

"Capri, stop playing. I need to pee, girl."

I laughed some more. "What you want me to do? I'm not untying you."

He gave me an odd look as if he didn't understand. "What the—"

I leaned closer in his face. "You're NOT leaving this chair or this room! Got it?"

Just then, I heard one of my neighbor's doors shut. I went to the door to peep out. It was the man across the hall. He didn't seem to be bothered by anything going on in my room because he checked his door to make sure it was locked then headed for the elevator. I figured I better turn on the TV to drown out Tremaine's voice. No one needed to know he was in my room.

After turning up the volume on the TV a bit, I stepped back over to Tremaine. His eyes said he didn't know what to think. He might've still been drunk. His words didn't slur though.

"Capri, c'mon, man. Time out for playin' and shit."

"You want me to slap your ass again?" I said, only inches from his face, holding my hand up. "Huh?"

"Naw. Hell naw!"

"Then recognize a lady when you see one! I'm not your fucking *man*."

"A'ight, damn! Now let me go. I told you I need to pee."

I backed out of his face then glanced around the room. I headed to the kitchen area then raked through the garbage bag and pulled out an empty water bottle then walked over to him.

"Pee in this."

"What?" He frowned.

"Don't act like you haven't done it before, hell." I unscrewed the top then kneeled to grab his penis. "Here, now pee."

"You're serious, huh?"

"Look, either you pee in this or pee on your self. If you're going to pee in this bottle, then I suggest you hurry up because I told you I've got things to do."

He sighed then began to urinate. At first, only a few trickles came out. He seemed to be having a hard time getting a steady stream. I threatened to take the bottle back twice, but after the third try, he released his urine until he was done.

"See, that wasn't so bad, was it?" I said, screwing the top back on the bottle.

"I can't believe this shit, to tell you the truth."

"Well, believe it." I headed for the trash.

"Man—" he cut himself off as I quickly spun around. "I mean, Capri . . . uh, my wife is probably wondering where I am."

I tossed the bottle into the garbage. "Let me see." I headed over to the nightstand to get his phone. "Eleven missed calls," I said, glancing at the screen. "Do you call her Baby Doll?"

"Yeah," he answered, trying to see over his shoulder.

"Yep. You're right. All eleven missed calls are from her." I laughed.

"This ain't cool. Yo', Capri, untie me. I've got to get out of here. She's probably having a fit right now."

"Oh, well. When I'm done with you, she can have you."

"What do you want from me?" he yelled.

I walked over and stood in front of him. "Now, we're talking. I want one hundred thousand dollars."

He looked more confused than he was before. "Do what?"

"I didn't stutter, Tré. Isn't that what the Missus calls you? Tré?"

"A hundred thousand dollars? Are you serious?"

"How many times do I have to tell you that I am?"

"I can't get you that kind of money."

"Yes, you can, and you will."

"How am I supposed to do that? If I withdraw that kind of cash, red flags will go up."

"I don't know how you're going to get it done. I just know that you *will* get it done. Or else you will wish you had never met me."

"I already wish I—"

WHAP, WHAP

I slapped him across one cheek with an open palm, and then across the other cheek with the back of my hand. The licks came so fast, he didn't have time to think about what was happening. He screamed, "Shit!" once it was over.

"You will watch your tone and what you say while you're with me, understand?" My voice was stern.

He looked as if he wanted to kill me, but he nodded slowly. "Yeah."

"Good. Glad that's cleared up. Now, while I'm gone, take time to figure out how you're going to get that money for me, a'ight?"

He nodded again. "Where are you going?"

"That's none of your business, but I'll leave the TV on for you. I might even bring you some breakfast back. But hear me, and hear me well: If I come back here and find that you tried something stupid, trying to escape, I will starve your ass and leave you here to rot. Got it?"

"Got it."

I went to get dressed, but before I left the room, I not only secured the scarf around Tremaine's mouth, but I also blindfolded him. The muffled sounds he made let me know he protested the blindfold, but hell, what could he do? I tried to make him feel better.

"Listen, don't fight it. This is best for both of us. This way, you won't get tempted to try to get away. I'm leaving the TV on as I stated, so you can listen to some music videos. Now be a good boy while I'm gone."

I eased out of the door, locking it behind me. I went to the beauty supply store to get a new wig, and then I needed to buy a few more outfits, so I'd have something sexy to wear for my boss. After all, Robin, I mean, *I* was Cole's new assistant, and I needed to look good for work.

Cole

27

*A*udrie left the house this morning without saying good-bye. Shawna and Gavin bid me a great day, but once they were packed and into the car, Audrie drove off as though she didn't see me standing in the doorway with pleading eyes.

There was no way to make things right between us. I couldn't blame her for not wanting to speak to me. I wouldn't speak to me either, if I were her. The scary part was not knowing where we would go from here. I still wanted my marriage, but given she wasn't speaking to me, I didn't know if she did. I could only pray for yet another chance.

Audrie didn't bother to fix enough breakfast for me. She and the kids ate, and then I was left to fend for myself. I toasted a bagel and made some coffee. When I saw the headline on The Commercial Appeal, I realized why Audrie had an even worse attitude than she did the night before. My name and Karma's picture was plastered all over the front page with a drama-filled story to follow about the incident at the club and such.

Audrie must've been seething when she saw this. She would have to face her coworkers and friends after this news. There was no more privacy. Our life was exposed for all to see. I went to glance out the living room window, looking for more reporters, but there didn't appear to be any out there. Maybe all the rain had kept them away. I closed the curtains then went back into the kitchen.

The paper lay on the table, and I couldn't resist picking it up. I read the story. It alleged that Karma and I carried an ongoing affair that resulted in a pregnancy before she was locked up. I was livid. No matter what I said to the media, they still made Karma's actions out to be about an affair she and I had before and during my marriage to Audrie. The storyline also refreshed readers on how Karma had been the one who killed Glenda.

I shouldn't have read that story. Now I was upset, too. I lost my appetite. I left the kitchen then went into my bedroom to get ready for work. *Poor Audrie*, I thought, fanning through the hanging shirts in my closet. I wondered how she would make it through her day with so much on her mind.

I decided to go in to work a little early. I hoped to be the first to get there, so I'd already be in my office and avoid the glaring eyes of my staff. The security officer in the lobby was the first face to greet me.

"Hey, Tom. How's it going this morning?" I asked on my way to the elevator.

"All is well, Mr. Patterson. How about you?"

"I'm hanging in there. Thanks for asking." I pressed the elevator button.

"Um, Mr. Patterson," he called.

"Yes, Tom?"

"Did you bring your morning paper for me?" he asked.

I left the paper behind on purpose. "Oh, no, Tom. I apologize. In my rush this morning to beat the new storm on the way, and I forgot the paper on the kitchen table," I lied. "Sorry about that."

"Oh, that's okay. I have a magazine. I'll just take a look at that until things pick up around here."

The elevator doors opened. "Okay, well, have a great day, Tom," I said, stepping inside.

I was right. I was first in my office to arrive. I knew I would be once I arrived and saw there were only a few cars in the lot. Most of my staff parked on the lot rather than in the garage. I walked inside my office, locked my door then went behind my desk and closed my eyes. I hadn't turned on the lights or my computer. I needed to clear my head before starting my day.

My peace was interrupted by my ringing desk phone only a few minutes into relaxing. I sighed deeply, hoping it wasn't Audrie, calling to give me another piece of her mind. I checked the caller ID. It wasn't Audrie. The number was unavailable, which more than likely meant it was a client calling from another state. I cleared my throat then answered the phone.

"Essential Software Development. This is Colby speaking. How may I help you?" There was silence on the line. "Hello? How may I help you?" I repeated. Still silence.

I hung up the phone, thinking there must've been a bad connection. Then, it rang again. The number was listed as unavailable. I figured it had to be the same caller.

"Hello, Colby speaking," I said into the receiver. Silence once again. This time, I felt sick to my stomach.

I hung up and waited to see if the phone would ring again. It did. I let it ring several times before picking it up and holding it to my ear. I didn't bother saying hello. My gut told me this was no client on the other end—it had to be Karma. I just held the phone, waiting to see if she would speak. Finally, the feminine voice chimed through.

"Cole!" she yelled.

"Huh, what? I mean, hello?"

"Cole, what are you doing?"

"Um, nothing, sweetie. I thought . . . um—"

"You thought what?" Audrie asked.

"Well, um, well, the number was listed as unavailable, and you didn't say anything, so—"

"That's because I'm used to the person on the other end saying hello first. I didn't know what was going on."

"What's wrong with your phone? Why isn't the number showing in the caller ID?"

"I don't know. I'm at work," she said.

"At work? What are you doing at work, sweetie? You should still be out on leave."

"No. I decided to come back," she said softly.

"Have you cleared everything with the human resource department?"

"Yeah." She sounded solemn.

"Sweetie, are you okay?"

"Yeah. I'll be alright. I would've called you when I first got here, but the lines were down. I just picked up the receiver a minute ago to see if there was a dial tone. What about there? Is everything up and running?"

"Um, yeah. Yeah . . . everything seems to be in great working order." I could hear her, but my mind was still shaken at the thought of how I'd thought Karma was playing games.

"I'm surprised you answered. I didn't expect you to be at work already."

"I'm here, but I haven't started my day. I'm just sitting here, relaxing with the lights off."

"Are you okay?" Her voice genuinely sounded concerned.

"After our fight last night, and that paper this morning—"

"So, you saw it?"

"Did I? I want to be okay, but . . . Audrie, I just don't know. I'm starting to feel like I'm in a bad dream."

"Then imagine how I feel."

I sighed. "I know, sweetie. I *have* imagined how you feel. It doesn't feel good at all. I've got to figure out how to make things right."

"Cole, there's nothing we can do. We're not bounty hunters. We can't go chase the girl down. The police are going to have to do their job."

"There has to be something—"

"Cole, don't go there. I don't like you very much right now, but you're still my husband. And I love you. That girl is dangerous. Let the police do their job."

Those words made me realize why I loved Audrie so much. I had to be the luckiest man in the world to be with a woman who could forgive me after messing up the way I did. I didn't say anything because I was thinking of how much I loved and appreciated her. My silence must've scared her.

"Cole, are you okay?"

"Yes . . . yes, sweetie. I'm fine. I'm sorry. I was just thinking of how much I love you, too."

"You owe me, Cole."

"I know . . . for the rest of my life—I'll forever be trying to make this up to you."

"I need to get some work done, and so do you. Turn your lights on, and get your day started."

"I will, sweetie. I love you, Audrie."

"I love you, too, Cole."

We hung up, and then the phone rang almost as quickly as I'd placed it on the receiver. I was shocked, wondering how she'd redialed the number so quickly.

"What did you forget to tell me, sweetie?"

"That you are my life, and I won't live without you, baby."

I stiffened, and my blood prickled as it ran through my veins like thousands of tiny needles. Audrie hadn't called me back. It was Karma. I was frozen and had no comeback for her. She must've known I was in shock because she didn't hang up or call my name. She just laughed and blew kisses into the phone. When she spoke again, she sounded as if she was about to purr.

"I love you so much, darling. I want to see you. When can I see you?"

My blood warmed once again. "Stay the fuck away from me. Do you hear me?" Her response was more laughter. "If you come near me or my family again, I swear—"

"You swear what, Cole? You want me, and you know it. You enjoyed me the other night. Admit it. You wish I was in Audrie's place, don't you? Don't worry, baby. I'm going to take care of her. Soon, she won't be in our way, and we can get custody of our daughter and live happily ever after. You'd like that wouldn't you?"

"Stay the fuck away, and I mean it!" I slammed the phone down.

After several more phone wars with Karma, I decided to take the phone off the hook. I tried to get some work done, but I was still distracted by thoughts of her taunting my family in the days to come. Why can't they find her? I thought. Something had to be done. Audrie and I were being tortured emotionally. This just couldn't go on.

An hour later, I managed to get into the groove of working, but that groove was soon interrupted by Tom pounding on my office door and screaming my name.

"Mr. Patterson," he called, out of breath. "Mr. Patterson."

I jumped to my feet and hurried to the door. "Tom," is everything alright?"

"Mr. Patterson, I've been trying to reach you on your phone." He sounded as if he'd trotted the four flights of stairs instead of using the elevator. "You have to come outside."

I panicked. "What is it? What's the problem, Tom?"

"Your car, sir. The alarm started blaring, and when I went out to see what the problem was, there was a young lady—"

I didn't let him finish. I darted by him, nearly knocking him into the doorframe as I headed toward the elevators. I pressed the button only twice, and when neither opened, I made a dash for the stairs. I heard dozens of rapid feet behind me, but I didn't look back. The way I took off running, I knew Tom and my entire staff were on my heels.

I made it outside only in time enough to hear screeching car tires, and then a large boom. I couldn't see the wreck on the main street from our parking lot, but I knew someone had crashed. I ran pass my own car as the alarm continued to blare, hoping to get a glimpse of what happened on the street. My guess was that Karma sped out of the lot into oncoming traffic and was hit by another car and disabled from leaving the scene.

I was wrong. She had caused two other cars to collide. Two men got out of their cars, shaking their fists at a blue Honda Accord as it burned rubber, leaving the scene. I didn't get a good look at the driver, but it was definitely a woman.

Karma

28

A change of plans—I couldn't get Cole to listen to anything I had to say, so I had to vamp the place. I thought I could get him to hear me out, and once he did, I was going to go up to his office and surprise him with a visit. Given that I look so much like Robin, I was sure the security guy would let me in. But, that Cole—my man—was so stubborn. He even had the nerve to take his phone off the hook. I couldn't even leave him a voice message because that stupid phone kept giving me a busy signal.

I headed back to my hotel, wondering how Cole liked how I'd tricked out his car with those bricks. I drove down to a nearby construction site and stole some of their bricks. I wasn't spotted because nobody was there. I guess the site was closed due to the rain.

When I entered my room, Tremaine was still intact. He was very still. I didn't know if he was scared to move or just sleeping. I walked over to him then untied the blindfold. He squinted and blinked multiple times as though it was hard for his eyes to focus. I removed the scarf around his mouth and asked how he was doing.

"How you think I'm doing," he said. I laughed. "This shit ain't funny, Capri. Let me go!"

"Ssshhh." I pressed my finger to my lip. "Not so loud or else I'll have to cover your mouth again. I'm going to release you—as soon as I get the one hundred grand we discussed."

"I told you I can't just withdraw that kind of money."

"And I said you can. You had an assignment while I was gone. Now what did you come up with?"

"Shit."

"Excuse me?"

"I didn't come up with shit. You ain't getting a hundred grand from me. As a matter of fact, your money well just ran dry. I'm done fucking with you after this shit."

I laughed. "Really?"

"Yes, really."

"You really think so?"

His eyes were curious yet strange. "Yeah. I know so."

I slowly walked over to the kitchen then picked up the butcher knife I purchased. I did a slow pivot and faced him. His eyes widened as I inched toward him, placing one foot in front of the other.

"You haven't figured out who I am, have you, Tremaine?" The knife was at my side.

With eyes as big as golf balls, he said, "No, but I do know you're crazy as hell."

I chuckled then cut it short and straightened my face. "That's what they tell me, but you might want to be careful about saying that again. I'm very sensitive about people calling me crazy."

"Look. Whatever I did to you, I'm sorry. Just let me go, and we can forget any of this ever happened."

I was inches from his face. "What *don't* you understand about me not letting you go?" I pulled back. "I gave you ample time to figure out a plan to get my money, but you fail."

His eyes followed the length of my arm, down to the knife in my hand. "So, what are you going to do? Kill me?"

"Yes," I said plainly.

At first his eyes widened some more, but then he collected some balls from somewhere and narrowed his eyes. "A'ight. Do it. Just kill me then."

I smiled and winked at him. He stared at me with a straight face. I could tell he didn't really think I was capable of murdering him, but I was about to remove all doubt from his mind. I set the knife on the dresser then went to the kitchen and fixed a small glass of orange juice. I knew he thought he'd called my bluff when he got cocky.

"And what happened to my food, woman? You said you would bring me back something to eat."

"I did say that, didn't I?" I said over my shoulder. I turned and walked toward him. "Drink this orange juice."

He frowned. "I don't even like orange juice."

"Everybody drinks orange juice."

"I'm not everybody." He was still smug.

"Well, it's all I got for now. Just drink it. It'll curve your appetite."

"How the hell am I supposed to drink it with my hands tied behind my back?"

"Here. I'll hold the glass for you."

I tilted the glass to his lips as he drank the juice non-stop. After his last gulp, he frowned and smacked his lips.

"Damn, girl, what kind of orange juice was that?"

"The kind I made up for you last night while you were out of it."

He coughed. "What? Did you poison me?"

"Don't worry. It won't kill you."

"What is it?"

"You'll find out in less than thirty minutes."

"So full of games—damn!" he said. "What's that supposed to mean?"

I shook my head then secured the scarf around his mouth. "Stop asking so many questions and just let it flow."

I went into the bathroom then took off my wig and fixed my hair. Tremaine probably had a million things going on in his mind, but he was in for the shock of his life. I refreshed my makeup before I stepped out of the bathroom about twenty-five minutes later. I was butt-naked.

Tremaine turned to look at me. His eyebrows rose. He seemed surprised at my new look, but I was confident he still didn't know about me. He shook his head.

"I can't believe this shit. You gone have me come over here for this bull—"

"Shut up!" I yelled.

I reached under the bed and pulled out a newspaper. I walked over to him then slammed it on his lap.

"What's this for?"

"You dared me to kill you as if you didn't think I was capable of doing it."

"And?"

"And I just wanted you to know who you're dealing with before I end your life today."

He lowered his head to his lap and saw my face along with a headline regarding my escape from the mental institution. He kept his eyes plastered on the story. I knew he was reading it because he gasped every few seconds. When he lifted his head and stared into my eyes, he looked as if he'd seen a ghost.

"What's d'matter?" I asked. "I don't hear you talking bad now."

"Hey . . . hey . . . listen. Um—"

"I'm tired of listening to you." I cut him off. "You want to die, and I have no problems helping you with that. You're lucky though. You're going to die a happy man because I'm going to ride your pony just to give me something to remember you by."

He frowned. "Man . . . I mean, Capri, I can't even get it up for you right now. I'm too stressed. You gon' have to let me go lay on the bed or something."

I smiled as I peered toward his midsection and saw the paper rising. He glanced down, too, and seemed amazed.

"Nice try, Tremaine, but I've already made sure you would get an erection. And it's right on time."

I snatched the paper away and began stroking him. He moaned a little then complained.

"Capri . . . uh, uh Karma . . . whatever the hell your name is," he said, obviously remembering the name he read in the newspaper. "What did you do to me?"

"I made sure you would rise to the occasion—literally," I answered, stroking him harder.

I took him into my mouth. He panted, moaned and cussed me out all in one breath.

"Oh, yeah . . . mmm . . . damn it, Capri, get your ass off me." His head was back and his eyes were closed.

"My *ass* isn't on you yet, but my mouth is."

"Oooohhh, yeeeeaaahhh. Mm-hmm. I mean it, Capri—uh, Karma. Get the fuck off me!"

I continued to take him deep into my mouth—long enough for him to get a throbbing, rock-hard erection, and then I climbed on top of him. I swirled my hips and used him like my love slave. There was nothing he could do about it.

Forty-five minutes and three orgasms later, I wasn't done with him. I bounced, up and down and round and round on him while he begged for mercy.

"Capri, that's enough," he said. "This shit hurts. I'm sore."

I ignored his pleas until I got my fourth orgasm, one hour into the escapade. I climbed off him. Tremaine seemed relieved. He climaxed at least once. I couldn't be sure about any other times because his moans and breathing were the same throughout. He wouldn't take his eyes off me. I was pretty sure he wanted to know what was next.

"So, are you ready?" I asked, picking up the knife.

"No! Capri, listen. I don't wanna die. I'm sorry. You were right. I just said that to get a reaction out of you."

"Oh, you've got one."

"No, Capri. I mean, Karma. I mean . . . what do I call you? Just listen. I do it."

"Do what?"

He panted. "I'll get the money. I swear."

I flashed him a broad smile. "You better not be pulling my leg."

"I'm not. Just let me call my agent. My agent can get the money out of the bank for me."

"Now let me tell you something: No games, you hear me?"

"I hear you."

"I'm serious Tremaine. I'm going to put him on speaker phone. No talking in codes and make sure he thinks he's dropping the money so that a friend will pick it up."

I gave Tremaine other instructions about where and what time to ask his agent to meet me. The agent was extremely concerned. He kept asking Tremaine if he was sure about this. I signaled Tremaine to wrap up the call then I placed the phone back on the nightstand where he couldn't get it.

I went to shower and change into something more befitting for the workplace. I put on the business suit I purchased before heading to Essential Software this morning. By late afternoon, I would be one hundred thousand dollars richer, but first, I needed to figure out a way for Cole and I to be face to face again.

Cole

29

*T*he police came. At least ten cars were there in record timing, but Karma was long gone, and so was the rain. The sky was still gray, but the air was dry, which was a good thing since all of my windows were gone. A few of the officers walked over to me.

"Are you the one who called?" one of them asked.

"Yes. I'm Colby Patterson."

"I understand you spotted Karma Jolley on this property," he said.

"Spotted her?" I asked. "I didn't actually see her, but I know it was her who busted up my car," I said, pointing. "Perhaps you can speak with my security. He might've gotten a good look at her."

"Alright, Mr. Patterson. I'm going over to take a look at your car while some of us have a talk with both you and your security."

"Thank you," I said.

"Oh, by the way," he turned and said. "The detective on your case is on his way."

"That's great, because this lady isn't going to stop." I shook my head. "She'll definitely have to be stopped."

"Mr. Patterson, you aren't thinking taking matters into your own hands, are you?" Another officer asked. "That is a no-no, and it could be very dangerous."

"Then, all I ask is for you guys to do your job before she hurts me or someone in my family. I can't allow my family to be hurt."

"I understand, Mr. Patterson. I'm sure nobody assigned to this case is sitting idly by while this woman disrupts your life," he said. "If it were that easy to catch her, she would've been caught a long time ago."

I glanced toward my car. Police and detectives surrounded it. They dusted my car and the bricks Karma used to bust the windows for fingerprints. A police helicopter flew above our heads, combing the grounds for Karma's vehicle in case she was still nearby. I wasn't hopeful that fingerprints would be found because Karma always knew how to out think people.

I spent an hour outside with the detectives and another hour inside the building as they questioned Tom about what he knew and me about the harassing phone calls to my desk. I felt some sense of hope when I was told an attempt to trace Karma's calls would be made. One police cruiser was assigned to circle the area until Karma could be caught. One thing was apparent—she would certainly try to see me again at any cost.

Once the police were gone and things quieted down again, I sat in my office and called Audrie to give her the update. She was very upset.

"That's it, Cole. I need a gun and a license to carry . . . now how soon can you help me get it?"

"Oh, uh, well—"

"We can't beat her at her games. We can't even fig-ure her out. I just want to be ready to protect myself in case she makes another spontaneous showing at the same grocery store I'm in."

"I understand, sweetie. Are you sure you want a gun?"

"I'm positive—never have been so sure before in my life. My father used to take me to the shooting range with him before he got sick and died six years ago. I'm confi-dent I still know how to handle a gun."

"Well, okay. We can start looking—"

"Today," she answered, cutting me off.

"Yeah. Today . . . I mean, this evening when we get off work is fine."

"Good. I'm fed up with her."

"I know you are, sweetie."

"Cole," she called. Her voice was softer now.

"Yes, sweetie?"

She paused before saying, "Could you still live with me after knowing I've taken someone's life?"

My heart fell. "Could I live with you?" I asked.

"Yeah. I mean, could you live with me and still love me?"

"Audrie, why are you asking me this? Have you killed someone before?"

"No, baby, I haven't. But I think I might real soon."

I sighed. "Karma?"

"Cole, I want her out of our lives just that bad. This is a living nightmare."

"Audrie, sweetie . . . maybe it won't come to that. But, for the record, I can and I will love you always—no matter what."

"Thank you, baby."

There was a long pause between us on the line. I could hear voices in Audrie's background so I knew she was still there. One of us had to end the awkward silence, so I spoke up.

"Sweetie, I haven't been able to get much work done today, so I need to get off the phone for now."

"Okay, babe. Do you think you'll be able to contact the building owners today about getting security cameras install on the lots for each location?"

"Um, yes. I should be able to get in touch with them today. I don't know why they haven't done that already."

"I know, right? Both places have cameras in the garages but not the parking lots."

"Yeah, that makes no sense. I'll give you a shout later to let you know what the owner said."

"Okay. Love you, Cole."

"Love you more, Audrie."

We ended our call then I placed the phone back on the receiver. The phone instantly rang back. I pounded my fist on the desk in anger. I was beyond sick of Karma and her mess. I snatched the phone off its base.

"Yeah!" I yelled.

No one said anything, so I slammed it down again. I thought about how Karma had played games on the phone earlier, so I quickly pulled the phone off the base again and set it on the desk. A fast beeping noise signaled that the phone was off the hook, but I waited patiently for it to stop. That receiver would not go back on the hook as far as I was concerned.

By lunchtime, Robin hadn't shown up for work or called. I tried to reach her cell phone, but it went straight to voicemail. I looked through her folder and found her emergency contacts. Her sister was listed as one. I placed the phone back on the hook then picked it up and listened for a dial tone. The line was clear, so I called the number.

"Hello," a soft-spoken woman answered, sounding like Robin.

"Hi, is this Robin Tyler?" I asked.

"No, but this is her sister, Kayla. How may I help you?"

"Hi, Kayla. This is Colby Patterson from Essential Software. I'm trying to reach Robin. She hasn't shown up for work since early last week. Is she alright?"

"Oh, Mr. Patterson. Thank you so much for calling. I'm at the hospital right now."

"Hospital?" I didn't expect this news, although I wasn't sure why, considering how long Robin had been off work.

"Yes, with Robin. She had been missing—probably since the last time you all saw her at work. She was found unconscious and not breathing in a dressing room at the Oak Court Mall."

"Oh, my God, is she okay?"

"The store attendant was able to revive her, but once Robin got to the hospital, she seemed to be having amnesia. The police didn't know who to contact. It wasn't until today that a security officer at the mall had the police run the tags of a car that had been left in the lot over a week that Robin's identity was discovered. Security and the hospital put two and two together."

My heart sank. Karma struck again. This had to be her doing. That would explain how she adapted Robin's look.

"Kayla, I'm so sorry to hear that. What hospital is she in?"

"We're at St. Francis Hospital. But, I just want to warn you in case you're thinking of coming here. She doesn't look as much like her normal self. She has a feeding tube in her stomach because the doctors say she kept taking the one out of her throat."

"I understand. Do you mind if I come visit her?"

"No, I don't mind at all. Maybe seeing you will help some of her memory. I'll be here for most of the day, so come whenever you can."

Kayla gave me all the information before we hung up. I called Audrie to update her and ask her to meet me at my office. Now, instead of feeling like I was only in a dream, my life felt more like a nightmare. If I didn't wake up soon, I was going to lose my mind.

Karma

30

I waited until the police car circled the parking lot of Essential Software and exited before I pulled inside. Many of the cars in the lot were gone, including Cole's. It was lunchtime. I wondered if he was gone for the day. After all, he did need to replace his windows before more rain came. I hated destroying his car like that, but how else would I get him to understand he needed to pay attention to me. Hanging up on me and not answering his phone when I call is not the smartest thing to do. I will not be ignored.

The police were probably keeping a close watch on the company, so I decided to pull into the garage to park. When I got on the elevator to go up on the ground floor to catch the next elevator, two women entered with me, holding bags from Taco Bell.

"Wow, that smells great," I said to them. "I haven't had Taco Bell in a while."

"Really?" one of them asked. "Well, the cheesy, double-beef burrito is back. That's the only reason I went today."

The other one laughed, and then said, "I know, right? I absolutely love all the items I can get there for under a dollar."

"Cheesy, double-beef burrito?" I asked. They nodded. "That sounds great. I'll have to try it next time."

As the elevator continued to the ground floor, the women started another conversation.

"I sure hope they catch that lady," one of them said.

"Yes, I know," the other one said. "What she did to that man's car is just awful. I'm not parking in the lot anymore until they catch her."

"You think he knows her?" the first lady said.

"Of course he does," I told them. "He's having an affair with her. He may never admit it though."

"Girl, I'm glad I don't work over in that office with you. Too much drama, if you ask me," the other woman said.

They thought I was Robin. I smiled inside, knowing this. This meant I would get away with whatever I wanted to do while Cole was out. The elevator doors opened, and we all piled out, heading for the next set of elevators. I was caught off guard when the security officer yelled out.

"Hey," he said.

My heart beat rapidly as I pressed the button for the elevator. I heard him scoot his chair out from his desk, but I still didn't turn around.

"Hey, um . . . um," he said, snapping his fingers. I could see him moving toward me quickly in my peripheral vision. I stared straight ahead. "Um . . . um, Robin!" I turned to him. "Yeah, that's your name—Robin. How are you doing?"

I swallowed hard, hoping my nerves didn't reek into my voice. "I'm great. How are you?"

The elevator doors opened and the other two women jumped on. I wanted to run behind them, but I was stuck listening to the old man.

"I'm great also," he said. "I haven't seen you around here in a while. Where've you been?"

I watch the elevator doors close. *Damn,* I thought. "Where've I been?" I asked.

"Yes. You've been on vacation or something."

"Yes—vacation. That's it. I've been on vacation." I pressed the button for the elevator again.

"Well, how was it?"

"It was nice."

He looked as if he wanted more. "So, where did you go?"

"Where did I go?" I asked, looking at the digital numbers on the elevator as they decreased. "Um, I didn't go anywhere. Sometimes it's just great to take some time off to do whatever, you know?"

"Oh, okay. I understand. Well, I'm glad you enjoyed your time off."

"Thank you."

The bell chimed, letting me know the elevator doors were about to open. The old man turned to leave then called me again.

"Oh, Robin. Mr. Patterson isn't in his office, so if you need to get in there, I have his key."

I smiled. The doors opened. I stepped in between to keep them from closing. "Oh, yes. I certainly need that key."

"Okay. I'll go and get it for you."

He walked over to his workstation, and then returned with the key. He handed it to me. I glanced at his name tag and pretended to know him.

"Thank you so much, Tom. I really appreciate this."

"No problem, Robin. Just don't forget to return it."

"Oh, I won't," I answered, releasing the elevator doors.

"Robin," he called. I pressed the button to the fourth floor. "I like the new hair," he said just before the doors closed.

"Thank you," I yelled, but I wasn't sure if he heard me.

When I got off the elevator onto Cole's floor, the entire area was practically empty. Tom was right. Just about everyone had gone to lunch around the same time. I could hear someone moving about in an office a few doors down from the one that had Cole's name on it. I moved slowly — careful not to alert the person of my presence. I eased the key into Cole's door then opened it without making a sound.

Once inside I had my way. Cole left his briefcase open on his desk. How perfect was this? I combed through his papers and found some very interesting items — files I knew he would need. I turned toward his computer monitor then moved the mouse. I laughed and shook my head. Mr. Intellectual actually left his computer up. The screen lit up and went right to a case he left opened as soon as I moved the mouse. I took the liberty to delete everything I thought that mattered on his computer. *That oughta get his attention.* I laughed some more.

I knew I needed to get out of there before he and the rest of the staff returned. I moved quickly. Once the elevator doors opened, I spotted Tom, standing just outside the entrance. He seemed to be watching the police circle the parking lot. *The key!* I thought. *I left it on Cole's desk. Oh, well.* I sneaked toward the garage elevator then pressed the button. I kept my eye on Tom until the elevator opened. I managed to get on without Tom noticing me.

I sat in my car for at least five minutes before pulling off. I drove out of the garage, hoping the coast was clear. It was. The police were no where in sight, and Tom no longer stood on the outside of the building.

As I exited the parking lot, I decided to call Audrie's cell—just to mess with her.

"Yeah," she answered after several rings.

"Yes, what?" I snapped.

"What do you want?"

"I've already told you—your husband . . . *my* husband, that is."

"Listen here, psycho! You pulled a sorry stunt with Robin Tyler, and it didn't work. I know you thought you killed her, but you didn't. She's alive."

"Well, good for her," I answered with a chuckle. *Damn,* was what I really thought.

"She's alive, and we're at the hospital with her now. As soon as she gets out of the hospital, she'll be testifying against you."

"I have to be caught first, right?" I was smug. Audrie didn't seem to know what to say. "I *won't* be caught, and I will live happily ever after with Cole and my children. Just make it easy on yourself, Audrie, and get out of my way. Cole doesn't want another upset like he had with Glenda, but as you can see, he got over her. He moved on with you, didn't he? And rest assured he'll keep having me whether you're around or not."

"Cole hates your ass. Look at all you've done. You murdered the mother of his kids, killed his best friend, and now all this other foolishness—"

"Cole loves me!"

"The hell he does!"

"Oh, yeah? Well, tell me this: Did you enjoy the video, Audrie?" She remained silent. "That's evidence of how much Cole really loves me."

Her words sounded as if they were from tight lips. "Don't you ever call me again, do you hear me?"

"And is that a threat, Audrie?"

"Yes, it is?"

"Good because I like threats. I'm fueled to do even more damage when I feel threatened." I laughed, and then she hung up on me.

I just had to call back, and when I did, Cole answered on the second ring.

"Karma!" he yelled.

"Yes, baby?" my voice was soft and smooth.

"Take your ass back to the nuthouse."

"Watch it, Cole. That bitch of yours has already crossed the lines when she called me psycho. You know how much I hate that, but don't worry. I'll fix her."

"Don't call her again. Do you hear me?"

I decided to be sweet. "Well, baby, I won't call her again if you just leave her and come be a family with me and our children. You know we have an infant who would love to meet you."

"That's not my baby, Karma, and stop saying that."

My blood began to boil. "Cole, it's your baby, and you know it is."

"You slept with Nick, too, Karma. Remember that?"

I sighed. "I know you weren't happy about that, baby, but he used a condom."

"That's not my baby, so get over it!"

He hung up on me. I was furious. I wanted to drive to every hospital possible, but that would be too many hospitals. I might not ever find him. Plus, I didn't want to hurt Cole. I only wanted to take care of Audrie and Robin. I could've sworn Robin was finished the first time.

The time on the dashboard of my car let me know it was time to meet Tremaine's agent with my money. The money would help me convince Cole we could be alright for a minute. He probably already had a significant savings, so one hundred thousand dollars on top of that would give us a great life, especially if Cole invested it. He could open his own software development company, and I would be right by his side. Yes. It was time to get our money, so I could be Mrs. Patterson once and for all.

Cole

31

We were in Audrie's car. I called her to follow me over to the auto body shop to drop off my car. After taking care of that, she and I drove over to St. Francis Hospital to check on Robin. Audrie couldn't believe the madness. We wondered if Karma had come into contact with Robin at my office and realized the slight resemblance then concocted a plan to steal her identity. We couldn't be sure until we spoke to Robin. Once we made it to the hospital, it was clear Robin was in no shape to talk. Audrie told Karma Robin would be testifying, but the truth of the matter was that Robin still had no memory of what happened to her. She whispered that I looked familiar, but she didn't even know me.

How one woman could be such a menace to society was insane in itself. Audrie would definitely be getting that gun she wanted. I couldn't let anything happen to her or my children. If I couldn't be around to protect them, they needed to be in a position to feel safe. Karma was clearly dangerous, and in this case, danger would have to be faced head on in order to overcome it.

Audrie pulled in front of my building to let me out. I gave her two soft pecks on the lips.

"Are you going to be okay until I get off?" Audrie asked.

"I'll be fine, sweetie."

"What about some lunch? We didn't stop to get any."

I shook my head. "I'm not hungry. My mind is spinning. I can't think about food right now."

"I know, baby, but you've got to eat something."

"Maybe when I leave work."

"So what time would you like me to come pick you up? I'm not going back to the office."

"You're not?"

"No, it's already four o'clock, and I signed out for half a day anyway."

"That was smart. Maybe I should've done the same thing, but I have something I was working on that I really need to finish today." I leaned over and kissed her lips again. "Just come and get me by five-thirty. That way, we'll still have time to get the children before the aftercare center closes."

"Okay. Good luck on the project."

"Thanks. See you soon."

I opened the car door then got out. I waved at her as she pulled off. A police car turned into the lot. I watched as the officer slowly drove down each aisle to inspect the area. At least they were doing that much to keep the area safe. There was no telling where Karma was at the moment. She seemed to have more smarts than she did craziness—or, did she? That stunt with Robin had me confused. Where did the strip club thing come into play? Did Robin work for the strip club at all, or was that something Karma added to Robin's resume as she stole her identity. All I knew was that I couldn't afford these distractions. I had too much going on at work already. One thing I could be grateful for was nearly being finished with the Hudson Engineering project. It only needed a few more touches, and then I could let one of the techs inspect it before it went out in a couple of days.

I walked inside and was greeted by Tom.

"Good afternoon, Mr. Patterson," he said just as I stepped in.

"Good afternoon, Tom." I stood in front of his desk. "Everything okay around here?"

"Oh, yes. Nothing out of the usual has happened since you left."

"Great. I'm glad to hear that."

"The police have been through here every fifteen minutes or so—like clockwork."

"Glad to hear that, too."

"I've been trying to keep an eye out myself. I don't know who that lady is, but she certainly came with an agenda. I'm just trying to make sure that agenda doesn't include vandalizing more of the employees' cars."

"She was pretty much after me, Tom."

"Oh, sir, I'm sorry. I didn't know that."

"I know you didn't. It's my fault. I should've filled you in. By the way, do you have an incident report in the drawer that I can fill out? You know the main office has to know about these things."

"Sure," he said, pulling open a drawer. "I see the missus dropped you off. Did you get your car squared away?" He handed me the forms.

"It's at the shop. It might be ready by late tomorrow, if I'm lucky."

"Well, I guess that's not too bad."

I tucked the papers under my arm. "I'll get this filled out, and then I'll need you to add your notations before I send it off in the morning. I know you had to write something for the police, and I'm very sorry you have to go through all of this."

"Oh, Mr. Patterson, it's no problem. That's why I'm here. It all comes with the job."

"Thanks, Tom."

I turned to leave, but he stopped me. "Oh, yeah, Mr. Patterson," he called.

I stopped and turned to look at him. "Yes, Tom?"

"Will Ms. Tyler be working late today?"

"Excuse me?" I could feel all the blood in my face drain.

"Ms. Tyler," he said.

I started back toward him. "What about her? She's been out for nearly a week."

"Oh, I know. She says she had a great vacation, too."

"Who?" I yelled. I didn't mean to, but I was stunned by what I heard.

He ignored my question. "Well, I asked because I was wondering if I need to stay late—until she gets off the clock since she came in so late."

I couldn't breathe. My nerves ran high. "*Who* came in late?"

"*Robin*," he blurted as if he wondered why I hadn't understood him before. "Ms. Tyler. What time is she—"

His words trailed as I dropped everything, including the incident papers, and ran for the stairs. The four flights came easy as adrenaline trickled my veins. I was out of breath by the time I reached my office door. I twisted the knob, and just as I had suspected, it was unlocked. I turned on the light and was surprised to see everything intact.

I hurried to my desk and hit the space bar. Nothing happened. I hit it again with my thumb. Nothing. I checked the power. The cord was disconnected. I bent under the desk to reattach everything.

"Come on, come on, come on," I said aloud.

Once I plugged the cord into the wall, I pulled myself up on my chair. I felt what seemed like a million eyes staring at me. My entire staff was hold up at my door and the small window to my office, staring at me. Tom made his way through the crowd.

"Is everything okay, Mr. Patterson?" he asked, out of breath.

"No," I answered through my own labored breathing. "That woman you saw wasn't Robin Tyler." I pressed the power button on the computer.

"What?" he asked.

"She was the same woman who vandalized my car."

"Oh, no. She didn't look the same."

"How did she look?"

"When she was in the parking lot, she had dark hair. But, she actually favored Ms. Tyler when she came in— only she had a shorter hairstyle. Oh, and it was auburn-colored. She held a conversation with me and everything."

"It was her alright," I said as I noticed the missing Hudson project.

Just then the phone rang. The caller ID revealed it was an unlisted number. I knew it had to be Karma. I sent everyone away.

"Show is over folks. I need to get this call," I told them.

"Anything you want me to do, Mr. Patterson?" Tom asked.

"Not right now, Tom." I fanned him away. "I'll call you back up in a minute."

As I picked up the phone, Tom backed out of my office and shut the door.

"Yeah," I answered.

"Hi, baby," she sang.

"Karma, the little stunts you pulled today aren't funny."

"They weren't meant to be funny, baby."

"Stop calling me your baby."

"Why, baby?"

I sucked in and exhaled a few good breaths. She found that funny. I wanted to hang up on her, but not before giving her a piece of my mind.

"Why do you need my project, Karma?"

"I don't need that project, Cole."

"Then why did you take it, and delete other programs, too?" I asked, noticing key elements missing.

"I wanted to get your attention. You won't listen to me. I just need you to hear me out."

"Well, guess what," I snapped. "I'm still not listening."

"You will, if you want your file back."

"Karma, you taught me a valuable lesson the last time you pulled that trick. What? You thought I didn't have a back up? Everything on this computer was backed up."

"Impressive, Cole. I'm thoroughly impressed."

"So, now what?"

"Notice anything else missing in your office?"

I sat up and looked around. "Everything is here."

"You think so?"

I glanced around the office again. "Yeah. I know so."

"Okay, then I guess I'll hang up now since you won't be listening to me. But, oh, wait. Once you figure out what's missing, how will you get in touch with me?"

"Why don't you quit the charade and just tell me what you think you have of mine that's valuable?"

"Would you happen to have another copy of that Hudson contract?"

I couldn't hold my surprise. I gasped as I ran over to my briefcase and saw that most of the contents were empty. It wasn't the contract I was worried about. I was more concerned about Hudson's confidential information being exposed. It was hard to tell if she understood everything in the contract and what leaking the contents would do to Essential Software and me. I remained calm.

"Karma, why so many games? This is not the way to get my attention."

"I don't know, Cole. I disagree. I think you would've hung up by now if you didn't care so much about my 'little stunts' as you call them."

"What do you want from me? I'm not going to leave my family, and you know that, so tell me what else do you want from me?"

"You don't have to leave your family—just Audrie, if you want her to live."

Anger surged through my voice. "Are you threatening my wife?"

"Calm down. Why are you so upset? It's not like I haven't threatened her before—or, that other one."

I couldn't say anything. I saw flashes of me with my hands around her throat, squeezing the life out of her. Audrie wanted me to let the police handle their job, but Karma had made one threat too many. At this point, I couldn't promise I wouldn't make an effort to find Karma on my own. I took a deep breath.

"I can't handle any more today. Call me on tomorrow."

"And then what?"

"I'll be more willing to talk and discuss a plan to see you, but you need to be ready to hand over the contract."

I could've sworn I heard a smile in her voice. "That's my Cole. I love y—"

I hung up before she could get it out. I closed out my computer for the day. I needed to leave, so I could come up with a solid plan overnight—one Karma wouldn't slink her way out of—and I was pretty sure I knew one that could work.

Karma

32

I'd had enough of aggravating Cole for the day. I hoped we would get to see each other, but that didn't happen. I was disappointed, but at least we ended on a good note. He agreed to think about seeing me. He wouldn't have to think long. Cole loved me. I know I stretched my actions to the limit sometimes, but he shouldn't have made it so hard to get his attention. I wasn't asking for too much. Cole was coming around, and soon we would have our happy ever after life.

It was time to get my money then head back to my hotel to check on Tremaine. I pulled into Overton Park and circled for nearly an hour. I had to make sure there were no traps set. I parked across from the entrance to the Memphis Zoo, but not too close. I didn't want to be easily seen as the drop would be made. Tremaine's agent was instructed to leave the bag of money on the sidewalk outside the zoo's parking lot. The agent didn't know I would be watching him. He was told the person in the parking booth would be picking up the bag from the sidewalk once he made the drop.

I didn't like all the questions his agent had, but Tremaine assured me the guy wouldn't do anything stupid. It was getting dark out when I noticed a small black car approaching slowly. I slid down in my seat. My heart pounded as I watched a guy pull over near the entrance of the zoo's parking lot then open his door. A dark-skinned man about 5'8 stepped out of a 300 ZX then tossed the bag onto the sidewalk. I was excited until I saw the bag hit the pavement. It seemed light—like it didn't have the money in it at all. I decided to stand back for a minute or two before driving over to get the bag, but I didn't have to because some stranger pulled up as soon as Tremaine's agent drove off. *What the—* I thought.

The car stopped just near where the bag had been thrown, and then a man got out of the car. This guy was even shorter than the agent. He looked to be around 5'6, medium complexion and a little stocky. I peered on as he opened the bag and swirled his hand around in it. Now it was apparent this man saw the agent toss the bag, so he stopped to be nosey. I wondered if he had my money. This guy was bold. He stood right where the bag had been dropped and searched it as if it had been left for him. After swirling his hand in the bag a few times, he began pulling out what looked like white tissue paper and throwing it to the ground. He seemed angry as he chunked the bag to the ground then pivoted toward his car.

He didn't make it into his car though. I nearly pissed on myself when the flashing blue lights and sirens whizzed by me and boxed the guy in. *It was a setup!* I thought. *Tremaine lied to me.* He told me he wasn't talking in codes with his agent, and that both he and the agent could be trusted. If I had been first to reach that bag, I would've been arrested.

I had Tremaine's phone with me. His agent was going to call it in case he needed further instructions. I turned off the phone and removed the battery. It dawned on me that if his agent sensed something wasn't right, he probably had Tremaine's cell tracked through the GPS. I wanted to get away from there, but I couldn't move.

It was a good thing his agent didn't expect a woman to pick up the money because as I sat looking on at the scene, it seemed as though the police were convinced they had their man. The man was handcuffed and placed in the backseat of one of the police cars while his car was searched. They were probably searching for Tremaine's phone. This whole fiasco took more than an hour to clear. I needed to stretch, but I dared not move until the coast was clear.

I couldn't wait to return to the hotel. Tremaine would pay dearly for this. There were no signs of police at my hotel when I got there. I parked then hurried inside. The entire building seemed empty. This made me nervous. I wondered if I was walking into another trap. I moved cautiously, set to flee the place, if need be. I made it to the elevator and up on my floor. Once I exited, I noticed even my hallway was still. I stood in front of my door and listened carefully. The TV was still on as I left it. Tremaine wouldn't be making noise because I left him tied down, blindfolded and gagged.

I opened the door and saw a terrifying sight. I hurried into the room then shut and locked my door. I searched the bathroom, the closet, and under my bed for intruders. I didn't see anyone. The sight that scared me so bad was Tremaine's body, toppled on the floor. He was still tied, blinded and gagged, but he was on his side, unmoving. I rushed over to him and removed the blindfold.

He blinked his eyes a few times, trying to focus. He seemed to be okay, but very disappointed to see me. He dropped his head and released an exasperated breath through his nose. He was heavy, but I managed to sit the chair up. I removed the gag and stared him head on.

"You tried to make enough noise to get somebody up here, didn't you?"

When he didn't respond, I pimp slapped him. This was twice he'd done something today to try to get me caught. I gave him an eye that let him know he was in a lot of trouble. I grabbed a bag and began to pack a few clothes and all of my money. I was sure Cole made the police aware that I attacked Robin, and too many people besides Cole and Audrie could identify me—that nosy old woman, Tremaine and his wife, Big Mike and the entire Sable Foxx staff. Tremaine looked at me.

"What are you doing?" he asked.

"What does it look like I'm doing?"

"You aren't leaving me here, are you?"

"Hell yeah. Where the hell would I take you?"

"You can't leave me here. I'm too weak. I'll die."

I laughed as I continued to pack. "You're going to die anyway."

His eyes widened. "What do you mean?"

I walked over to him. "You set me up, Tremaine."

"No, I didn't."

"Yes, you did. I said no games."

"But, I didn't—"

"Shut up!" I was stern. Tremaine didn't attempt to say anything else. "Do you really think I'm stupid?" I asked. He remained silent. "I know you think I'm crazy, but surely you can't think I'm stupid, too."

He shook his head. "I'm sorry."

"Too late. My name and face is all over the news, and I'm sure your wife and agent are frantically searching for you now that you've alerted your agent. Why would you do that?"

"I didn't think you were going to let me go."

"Well, now you know I'm not going to let you go."

"Look. Give me another chance. I'll make sure you get the money."

I walked away. "Ha! Trust you again? You've deceived me twice. I left here, and you tried to get me in trouble by throwing yourself to the floor. You should've killed yourself. You would've been better off."

"What happened to three strikes? Please. Just give me another chance."

"I'm not a woman of many chances—except when it comes to my man. But you don't know him. He's the love of my life, and all I wanted from you was a little financial help, so he and I could build our lives. Now you're useless."

"Naw, man—I mean, Capri. I still got that money you want. I'll make sure you get it."

"It's too late, Tremaine. I can't risk being in the public too much. I've got to find another hiding space until my man decides to help me. You had your chance to help me."

I walked over to the kitchen area. When I turned around Tremaine's eyes were glued to the object in my hand.

"Wwwhaattt are you going to do with that?" he asked.

I held a large, shiny, new knife in my hand. It was sharp and ready for slicing. I smirked as I moved closer. His voice rose as he began to plead for his life. Concerned that someone would hear him, I set the knife near the TV then gagged him. He closed his eyes.

"You can watch, if you want," I told him.

He shook his head, but when I grabbed hold of his penis then whacked it off with one swift, sweeping motion, his eyes automatically popped open. His screams were muzzled, thank goodness. Blood shot everywhere. It was all over me. I had to shower and change before I could get out of there. I dropped the severed muscle into his lap and left the knife on the floor.

After taking a hot shower and gathering my belongings, I walked over to take a look at Tremaine. He seemed to be going in and out of consciousness. I shook my head at him then walked out.

Cole

33

---

*A*fter Audrie picked me up from work, we took the children to Benihana's for dinner. We chatted about our plans for Karma while Shawna and Gavin were mesmerized by the chef's cooking. They applauded when he cracked an egg then tossed the shell into the air and caught it in his hat.

"Did you see that, daddy?" Gavin asked.

"Yes, I sure did, son. That was great."

I made sure to keep an eye on the chef while Audrie and I talked because I needed to make sure he kept all shell food and other items Gavin couldn't have away from the side he cooked Gavin's food on. Audrie kept a close watch, too, as we whispered.

"Cole, I'm only agreeing to this because you've promised me it will work."

I stroked her back. "Sweetie, it will be broad daylight, and there will be plenty of people around. Besides, you'll even be in hiding. If you see anything strange—"

"Alright, alright. I hear you. Now, if only you can get her to agree to it."

"She will. Trust me. She thinks I want to see her as much as she wants to see me. This will work."

After dinner, we headed home, but Audrie had no intentions of entering the house just then.

"Where're you going, sweetie?"

"I'll be back shortly, Cole, I promise," she said, backing out of the driveway.

She didn't give me a chance to protest. I watched her leave our driveway and head down the street. I wanted to go into the house and call her cell, but something told me she just needed some space. I glanced around the neighborhood. Everything seemed peaceful, but there were no police cars around. *Maybe they're combing my street in ten or fifteen minute intervals as they did at the office today*, I thought.

I took the children inside so they could start their homework. Audrie called an hour later, saying she was fine and that she would be home in half an hour. I showered and was in the bed asleep when she made it home. I was drained. I wanted to wake up to ask her about where she'd been, but I was too tired.

The next morning, we dropped the children at school, and then Audrie took me to work.

"What if she doesn't call?" Audrie asked before I stepped foot out of the car.

"C'mon. This is Karma we're talking about. She'll call."

"So, are you going to get your car this morning?"

"Yes. I'll call the shop as soon as I get in the office. If it's ready, I'll catch a cab to pick it up."

"Then, what?"

"Then, I'll be right back at the office, waiting for Karma to call."

"You'll keep me posted."

I sighed. "Sweetie, please don't worry. I can see your nerves are getting the best of you."

"I can't help it, Cole. This woman is relentless. I just want all of this to be over."

"And it will. Today. I promise."

Audrie tried to smile, but I could see through the mask. I had some concerns about our plan not working, too, but I wasn't nearly as worried as Audrie. I had to promise her things would go over well in order for her to even be a little bit okay with helping the police "do their job" as she'd put it.

I walked into the office about fifteen minutes after everyone else. Tom was posted at his station. I gave him the morning paper.

"Thank you, Mr. Patterson. I hope your morning is going well."

"I'm okay, Tom," I answered, heading toward the elevator. "Hopefully today won't be as eventful as yesterday."

"Well, I've got my fingers crossed for a better day, sir."

"Thanks. Me, too."

I stepped onto the elevator and rode to my floor. All seemed calm as I headed to my office. I bid good mornings to my staff before opening my door. Once inside, I could see the voicemail signal blinking before I turned on the lights. I flipped the light switch on the wall then walked over to my desk. I dialed the voicemail then let it play on the speaker as I logged onto my computer.

"Colby," an older voice said. "This is Ms. Willis," she said. I stopped what I was doing to listen to my former neighbor. "Please give me a call. I just got out of the hospital. I saw that ol' crazy girl—the one what killed Glenda. I saw her at the emergency room not long ago, and she said that you and her were married—said she was there to visit you. I knew she was lying though—'bout being married to ya. I knew that couldn't be the truth. Anyway, she knocked me down on this ol' bad hip. Bruised me up pretty bad, but I'll live. I'm home now, so give me a call so I can tell you what she look like. I see she wanted by the authorities. I'll tell y'all anything you need to know, so they can catch her. She still crazy, Cole. That girl ain't got a lick of sense. Call me. This is Ms. Willis."

She hung up. That was the only message on the voicemail. Karma had managed to surprise me again. I had no idea she tried to visit me at the hospital. I should've called Ms. Willis. She was like a mother to me. I felt terrible for not warning her that Karma had escaped.

Ms. Willis and I talked for half an hour. She filled me in on what happened at the emergency room, and I updated her on Karma's antics since her breakout. Ms. Willis wasn't scared of Karma.

"Let that girl come messing with me, if she wanna," she told me. "I got something for her!"

"Ms. Willis, I don't think you have to worry about Karma. It's me she wants to get."

"Colby, protect your family. I know you can't be 'round 'em twenty-four hours a day, but do the best you can, ya hear?"

"Yes, ma'am. I'm doing all I can."

"Good."

When the other line beeped, I recognized it was an unlisted number. I rushed Ms. Willis off the phone, stating I would give her a call a little later. It took us a minute to get off the phone, and I wondered if Karma would still be there.

"Essential Software Development. This is Colby," I said after pressing the button to the other line.

"Baby, I thought you weren't going to answer," she said.

"I'm at work, Karma. I do have to talk on the phone to other people sometimes."

"Why don't you just give me your cell phone number, and I won't have to bother you at work."

"Um, that would be a negative."

She gasped. "Why not?"

"Well, at least not right now. We have to get reacquainted first."

"Is that what you're waiting on? Baby, I still know you. Why don't you feel you know me?"

"Karma, you come out of a new bag every time we talk or see each other. You do too much."

"Alright. I'll tone it down. I just want you to know how much I love you."

"Well, I know."

I could hear a smile in her voice. "You do?"

"Absolutely," I lied.

"So, what's the deal? Do I get to see you today or what?"

"That's up to you."

"What do you mean?"

"I contacted the foster parents of our child," I said, still lying. I held my breath, wondering if she read me.

"Colbia? You found her?"

"Yes. I located her when I got off the phone with you. I contacted the foster parents, and I was allowed to visit her, too."

"You did? How is she?" Karma's voice reeked excitement.

"She's doing great. She really is a beautiful baby, Karma."

"She looks like you, doesn't she?"

I paused, unsure how to answer. "No. She looks like her mother." I wanted no parts of owning the baby.

"Aw, that's sweet, Cole. Thanks. I can't wait to see her again. She's grown, hasn't she?"

"Yes, and guess what."

"What?"

"You get to see her today, if you want."

"What?" Karma sounded as if she didn't believe me. "Really?"

"I told the foster parents to meet me this afternoon so I can see the baby again, but I didn't say where yet. I had to make sure you wanted to be there."

"Of course I want to be there, but those people won't let me be anywhere near that baby, will they?"

"I didn't tell them you would be there. I'm going to let you know the time and place, and you should just show up after we've been there for a while."

"Okay. How about Overton Park?" she asked, her voice still full of enthusiasm.

"Why Overton Park?"

"They should feel safe there. It's a public park."

"Well, okay. I guess we'll look for a place with a table or bench. I'll be sitting there with the parents and the baby."

"Cole, this isn't a setup, is it?"

I swallowed then answered. "What do you mean?"

"Cole, I just went through something with someone who tried to set me up. I want to trust you—"

"Karma, listen. I can imagine it's hard for you to trust me right now, especially with all the media about your escape and such, but you and I agreed to work something out so that we could see each other today. I thought you'd be happy to see the baby."

"I am happy."

"Okay, then let's make this happen."

"Alright."

"Hey, don't forget to bring the contract."

"Oh, so is that the only reason you went out of your way to find Colbia?"

I hesitated. "No. There's more to it." That wasn't a lie. Karma just had no idea how much more to my plan there was.

"Hmph. Alright."

"I'll call the foster parents back and let them know to meet me at four o'clock."

"I'll see you about 4:15."

"I look forward to it," I said then hung up.

And I meant that literally.

Karma

34

---

*C*ole made me the happiest woman in the world with the news of finding our daughter. I noticed, however, that he wouldn't call her our daughter or his baby. He would only call her "the baby." I didn't like that too much, but at least he agreed to see Colbia. I was excited about seeing them together. I knew once Cole saw how great we looked as a family, he would drop Audrie in a heartbeat. He was a family man, and Audrie had no blood ties to him like I did.

I went to buy some gym shoes and a jogging suit. All I needed was to get our baby, and then Cole would bring Shawna and Gavin along to join our family. I hadn't thought about where we'd stay or how we'd get by, given I didn't have the money Tremaine lied about giving me. It would be tough at first, but Cole was a smart man. He would never let his family struggle. We were going to be okay. I just knew it.

Instead of a wig, I brushed my hair to the back, and put on a black baseball cap. I headed to the park around 3:30 and did the same thing I'd done with Tremaine's agent in Overton Park—scoped the place before pulling over. There were a handful of people in the park. I saw a couple jogging, a family of four walked in the grass, and a few teens throwing Frisbees. I didn't see anyone who looked suspicious.

It seemed that I'd made it there before Cole. Then, I saw his car driving up. He glanced over to a picnic table area then pulled his car over. The car looked great, considering the amount of damage I'd done to it. He had it fixed in a hurry.

He got out of the car then headed over to the table. I watched him dial someone's number then place his phone to his ear. I was too far away to be able to read his lips. Now that I knew where he would be, I cranked my car then drove a few streets over, outside of the area, to park my car. I sneaked over behind some shrubbery where Cole sat at a table. I sat on the ground, peering at him through the shrubs. I could see a short, medium-complexioned woman walking up with a stroller. When Cole rose to greet her, he blocked my view of the woman and the baby.

He sat back at the table and the woman did the same. I saw the two of them playing with the baby in the stroller. The stroller's back was turned toward me, so I still couldn't see my baby. My heart raced. I wanted to see her so bad. I didn't make my move just yet because I needed to make sure no one else was with the woman. Her husband might've been parking the car or somewhere nearby.

She and Cole sat at the table chatting for a bit. I couldn't hear a thing they were saying. I wanted to move closer, but there was nothing for me to hide behind if I did. I sat just a few minutes longer, then got up, satisfied no one else was with the woman. I started toward Cole and the woman, but they were too engrossed in their conversation to see me.

Cole stood up, and so did the woman. That's when they both looked my way. Cole looked as if he wasn't sure it was me, but the woman looked as if she'd seen a ghost. She looked frightened by the sight of me. Cole said something to her, and then she turned to walk off with the stroller. She moved fast—faster than I'd ever seen a woman with a stroller move before.

My eyes darted to Cole. He looked poised to grab me. Another damn set up! I thought. I put my running shoes into action. I did a fake charge toward Cole. He stooped, ready for impact, but I did a spin and went to his left. The woman looked back and saw me coming. She screamed and broke away from the stroller. I headed straight for my baby. I pushed the stroller at full speed ahead. It was light. Too light, but I could see the baby as she lay motionless inside. She was covered to her neck with a yellow blanket, but I could see her curly, black hair and the side of her face.

Pushing the stroller on the grass slowed me down. I looked behind me, and Cole was gaining on me. When I turned and looked in front of me, Audrie was running toward me. She screamed at Cole.

"Stop her," she yelled. "Stop her, Cole!"

He yelled back at her. "Call the police, Audrie. Call the police now!"

She stopped her pursuit toward me and pulled out a cell phone. "Okay," she yelled, pressing buttons on the phone.

I knew I had to abandon the stroller if I was going to get away. I stopped then quickly reached into the stroller bed and grabbed the baby. I struggled to get her out because she had been strapped in. Once I released the straps, I snatched her up with so much force, I fell backward onto the ground. The baby was so light, she went tumbling a couple of feet from me. She didn't cry. In fact, she didn't make a sound. I panicked. I scrambled to my knees and reached for her. I could hear Cole running closer.

Once I had the baby in my arms, I realized why she hadn't cried. She wasn't a baby at all. She was a doll—with lots of hair. I rose on my feet. Cole was right up on me. I swung my hand back with the doll and popped Cole in his face. He fell backward. That was my chance to take off.

I heard sirens, but I ducked off toward my car, which was only three streets over. I looked back as I ran. Cole and Audrie sat on the ground. They were busy tending to Cole's face. He might've been bleeding because he kept wiping at his face.

I jumped in my car and quickly left the scene. Cole tricked me. He made me believe he wasn't trying to set me up. Didn't he know it wasn't good to make me mad? Or, maybe he just wasn't clear on why I broke out of the mental hospital in the first place. I didn't belong there. I belonged with Cole. Just like Tremaine, Cole would have to pay for his deceit, except I wasn't going to be violent toward him. Audrie was about to get it. He'd miss her for a while, but with her out of our way, he would be glad to move on.

Cole

35

*T*he police took our report and fussed about us taking the law into our own hands. The plan was to have Audrie's sister, Felecia, pretend to be the foster mother of Karma's baby—only the baby was a doll. Once Karma got close enough to me, I was going to grab her and hold her until the police came. But, somehow, Karma seemed to have figured me out. She got by me and headed straight for the stroller. She was quick. She should've run track in high school, if she didn't. Her speed was amazing. Or, maybe it was all coerced by her adrenaline. Either way, I fell short of catching her.

Just when I thought I had her, she flung that doll in my face so hard, I lost my balance. She left my mouth swollen and bleeding. I wouldn't let Audrie chase Karma. I held her on the ground with me until the police came. I never meant to involve the police until I had Karma securely locked on the ground. As I got close to her, I just knew I had her. That's the only reason I yelled for Audrie to call the police. Audrie let me have an earful in the car and once we made it home. I watched her pull all the mail out of the box then we walked inside.

"And the only reason I agreed was because you promised me, Cole," she said, closing the door behind her and locking it. "You promised me nothing would go wrong."

I plopped onto the couch. "I didn't promise that, Audrie."

"Okay, maybe those weren't your exact words, but you did say your plan would work."

"Audrie, I knew if I said anything remotely close to the fact that I *hoped* this plan would work rather than knowing it would work, you wouldn't have agreed to it."

She stomped and pouted. "Dang it! It was a good plan. How did we mess it up?"

"Sweetie, the look in Karma's eyes when she first came toward me let me know she was on to us."

"And where was the contract? She didn't have anything in her hands when she ran toward you."

"I noticed. I don't think she ever planned to give it to me. She's too smart for her own good."

"So, what are you going to do about the contract?"

"I'll come up with a reason the company needs to give me a new contract. Hopefully, Karma will be mad enough to just burn that one or rip it up."

Audrie shook her head. "I really wanted you to let the police handle their job, Cole."

"That girl is becoming more and more reckless. She's a threat to everybody. I'm tired of her games now. It's well-past time for her to be caught."

"I know, baby, but maybe we should've let the police in on what we were doing. You know if there had been enough of them in the area, surveying our plan, she could've been caught."

"Yeah, but I didn't want to run the risk of letting them in on our plan, and them telling us to stand back. I felt our plan would work more so than not."

Audrie plopped on the couch next to me. "I guess we should call the Clarks and let them know we're home, huh?"

I nodded and pulled her head onto my shoulder. "Sweetie, something will give. She can't run forever."

"Yeah, but the problem is that she thinks she can."

Audrie pulled her cell from her pocket then called the Clarks.

"Yes, ma'am," I heard her say into the phone. "Okay. That will be great. I'll let Cole know." She paused. "Alright, and thank you, Mrs. Clark." She hung up.

"What was that all about?" I asked.

Audrie sat up. "Mrs. Clark said the children asked if they could stay over. She says they have clean school clothes for tomorrow, and that she and Mr. Clark would get them off to school for us in the morning."

"What did you tell her?"

"I told her it would be fine. I hope that was okay with you."

I pulled Audrie back down on my shoulder. "I guess it couldn't hurt. I mean, they offered. It's not like we asked the Clarks to tend to the children all night. I hope they remember the children will be back over on the weekend."

"I'm sure they remember," Audrie said. "Hey, babe."

"Yes."

"Let's go back to Hot Springs this weekend—my treat."

"Hmm…that's tempting, sweetie, but I can't let you do that."

"Why not? I want to get away again. You don't think Karma will follow us, do you?"

I shrugged. "I don't know, but I rather do Gatlinburg or somewhere else in Tennessee this time."

"Oh, Gatlinburg sounds great."

"Great. I'll make arrangements in the morning." I sat up. "Is this the mail that came in today?" I picked up the pieces from the coffee table.

"Yes, I'm sorry. I totally forgot I brought that in."

I handed Audrie the mail with her name on it and placed all bills back on the coffee table. The last piece of mail had my name on it. My eyes must've looked like they were about to pop out of my head because it was the news I'd been waiting on. It was the DNA results of Karma's baby. Audrie noticed how my hand shook.

"Baby, what's wrong?" she asked, holding my trembling hand.

"This is it," was all I could say.

"What?"

"The DNA results."

"Open it, Cole."

I pulled the envelope closer to my face. "I'm scared."

Audrie stroked my back. "Cole, baby, look. We knew since getting that letter there was a fifty-fifty chance you are the father. I'm not going to lie." Her voice began to break with tears. "It's going to be hard to adjust to the idea that Karma has a baby with you, but I'm not going anywhere. I'll do whatever we have to do for that baby—including taking her in, if that's what you want to do."

I did a double-take at Audrie. Her tear-stained face was serious. It was clear she meant what she said. I dropped my head into my lap. I was hurt by the fact that the fate of the rest of our lives was on the inside of one small envelope. Whether the baby was mine wasn't that great of an issue. The bigger matter at the moment was the hurt that Audrie and I shared. Audrie was being made to suffer vicariously as a direct result of me having sex with Karma when I knew I would never have a long-term relationship with her—let alone wed her. I buried my face and cried. I cried for my past and my future. Audrie did her best to console me.

"It's okay," she said, her voice shaken with tears. "It's okay, Cole. Either way, I have forgiven you. For everything. I just want to move forward and have a great life, whatever that means, with you and our kids."

I rose and glanced at the envelope in my hands again. Audrie continued to stroke my back. Then, I opened the envelope and skimmed the letter for what I needed to know. Audrie must've spotted the words at the same time as I did because we both gasped and looked at each other. She had one last tear to fall from her eye. I wiped it away then locked my lips with hers.

We were both crying again as we kissed.

"I love you, Cole," she said between kisses. "I love you."

"Can you believe it?" I said, catching a breath. "I told you, sweetie." I kissed her again. "She isn't mine." Another kiss. "The baby isn't mine."

Audrie giggled and kissed me some more. Then, she caught her breath. "It's time to celebrate."

She stood and pulled me up by my shirt. "What? What are you doing?"

"I want you," she said, seductively.

"Sweetie, I need to shower. You forgot I broke a sweat in that park."

She continued to pull me. "We can shower together." She noticed I still had the letter in my hand. "Put this down." She took the letter and placed it on the coffee table. "Let's go, Mr. Patterson." She beckoned me with her finger.

"Coming, Mrs. Patterson."

Karma

36

Somebody forgot to lock the window in Shawna's room, making it too easy to enter the house. I thought getting pass the sleeping man in the guard shack was a piece of cake, but getting into Cole's house before the police patrolled the area again was just plain effortless. Once I was inside, I was disappointed to see that Shawna wasn't there, and neither was Gavin.

Shawna's room was beautiful. I wanted to turn on the light to take in all that was done to enhance the Princess and the Frog theme, but that would only get me discovered. I could hear Cole and Audrie talking in a room nearby. I sat on Shawna's daybed. It was covered with fluffy, pink pillows and pink-and-white lace. I sat in a daze, thinking back to the days when I was happy being spoiled as a little girl. Something smelled of a soft, lavender scent. I glanced over to her dresser and saw a decorated bowl of potpourri. My mother used to place potpourri in my room, too.

Cole's voice became louder. I walked over and slowly cracked the bedroom door. I wanted to see how close he was. I couldn't see very far into the hallway, but I could tell his room was only just up the hall. I wanted so badly to make my presence known. In due time, I would. I had to be strategic about my attack. Audrie couldn't know I was coming. I listened on to see what their plans were for the night.

"I can't wait to get you in that shower, Mrs. Patterson," I heard him say.

"Oh, yeah? And what are you gonna do to me?"

"I can show you better than I can tell you."

"Aaaahhhh! Is that right, Mr. Patterson?"

"You know it. I can back up everything I say."

"Oh, I know, and I can't wait."

"Then, stop talking and get your clothes off."

"Wait," Audrie said.

"What's wrong?"

"Do you think we ought to make sure the police are patrolling?"

"Sweetie, they are. Everything is locked up, so we'll be fine in the shower."

"Oh, so you don't plan on being in there long, huh?" She laughed. "I guess you know what you're dealing with, too."

"So true."

"I just might put it on you so good, you won't last."

He laughed. "Stop all your talking and get in the shower."

I heard the shower water running. I waited a couple of minutes to make sure they were in the shower before I headed out of the room. I eased down the hall and made my way into the living room. I noticed an entryway that looked as if it led to the kitchen. There had to be a weapon in there I could use. I hurried inside. I didn't turn on the light since I didn't know where all of the windows were. The police could spot me and blow up all of my plans.

It was hard to see in the kitchen. I opened cabinets and drawers, and I still didn't find the right weapon. After searching a few more drawers, I finally decided on a knife. I headed back into the living, and then toward the hallway that led to the bedrooms. On my way to the hall, I spotted some open mail on the coffee table. Since I knew Cole and Audrie would be in the shower for a while, I decided to pry.

I took a seat on the couch and set the knife on the table. I picked up the letter and read it. My eyes zeroed in on a certain section. It read:

based on the dna analysis, the alleged father, colby patterson is excluded as the biological father of the child, colbia jolley, because they do not share sufficient genetic markers. therefore, the probability of paternity is 0.0%.

My jaw damned near hit the floor. I tossed the letter back onto the table. I couldn't believe what I read. *How could this be? Cole has to be the father. How could he not be the father? Unless—Nick?* I gasped. I held my head and shook it. Not Nick. No, not Nick!

I jumped from the couch. I stared at the knife. I was more furious now than I'd been before I came over there. Cole deceived me at the park, and now he had confirmation to the news he'd been claiming all along—that Colbia was not his daughter.

I thought back to moments before, when I heard Audrie's happy voice in the other room with my man. The knife was tempting, but given Cole was in the house, I didn't want to take a chance on him getting the knife from me and using it to hurt me. I headed toward their bedroom, determined to do what I had to do to Audrie—with my bare hands.

I eased into their bedroom. They were still in the shower, and they had no idea I was there. When I cracked the bathroom door, I wanted to close it immediately. I couldn't see them, but the sounds of Cole making love to her was sickening. I couldn't breathe. I wanted to charge them right then and there, but I couldn't move. I stood, listening as they finished.

"Oh, Cole, you were wonderful!" she said.

"And so were you, sweetie."

I heard smacking noises as if they were kissing.

"What? You want some more of this, don't you?" Cole said.

"Yeah, but that's not why I looked at you. I don't know why, but suddenly, I feel a sense of relief."

He laughed. "Um, yeah, I guess so. You seemed to have reached the greatest climax of your life." He laughed some more. "And I'm just glad I had something to do with that."

"Baby, all of that is true, but that's not the reason I feel at ease right now."

"It's not?"

"No. I guess now that we have the DNA results—and it's negative—I'm more hopeful that Karma will leave us alone."

"Let's just pray, sweetie. That's all we can do."

"I know." More lip smacking.

I was so disgusted, I hit the wall before I knew it. I wasn't sure if they'd heard me over the shower, so I eased the door closed and listened closely.

"What's wrong?" Cole asked.

"Ssshhh. Did you hear something?"

"No, sweetie. You think you heard something?"

"Cole, I know I did."

"C'mon. Let's get out of here," he said.

I got out of their bedroom as fast as I could. I needed to hide. I couldn't let them discover me before I made my surprise move on Audrie. As far as I was concerned, she had just enjoyed her last night with my man. He would be mine from now on.

Cole

37

---

*A*udrie and I barely got all of our clothes off before we made it into the shower and had celebratory sex. My sweetie was happy for a change, and it felt great having her in my arms. Her soft, perky breasts pressed firmly against my chest as the warm water pummeled my back. I lifted her leg onto my arm and entered her place of warmth. She planted her hand on the wall and wrapped her other arm around my neck. We locked lips and sent jolts of passion through each other for the entire lovemaking session.

We exploded at the same time. Audrie released harder than I can ever remember. She could hardly stand. I held on to her, planting several soft, sensual kisses over her face and neck. It took us a minute to catch our breaths, and then we washed each other. Shortly after rinsing the soap from our bodies, Audrie heard a strange noise, so we hurried out of the shower.

Audrie dried herself as I threw on my robe and went to inspect everything. I checked the windows and the doors. They all were still secure, but the alarm hadn't been set. In our haste to get to the shower, Audrie and I forgot to set the alarm. I set it then headed back to the bedroom and closed the door.

"Everything alright?" Audrie asked just as I walked in. She sat on the side of the bed, applying lotion to her legs.

"Yeah. Everything is fine." I closed the door behind me because with Audrie's nerves, she would probably jump all night, thinking she heard something.

"Great." She stood to put on her nightgown.

"Um, you can put that back in the drawer. You won't need that tonight."

She smiled, but still slipped the gown over her head. "Well, that's good news, but you know how I am. I need to feel something next to my skin as I sleep."

I went over and wrapped my arms around her waist. "I've got something you can feel next to your skin."

She popped me on my shoulder. "You know what I mean." We shared a brief kiss. "Cole, I need to ask you something."

"Uh-oh." I released her waist. "Hold on. Let me take a seat." I sat on the bed. "I did need to take a seat, right? I could see it on your face."

Audrie sat next to me. "Yeah, but this is not an 'uh-oh' moment. At least, I don't think it is."

"Okay, then what is it?"

"How do you feel about us increasing our family?"

I wondered what brought on this question. "Are you asking me this because of Karma and her baby?"

"No. No, that's not it?"

"Oh. I thought maybe you were asking me this because somehow you had gotten used to the idea of Colbia possibly being mine, and now you want a baby."

"No. Hell, no. Cole, you have no idea how relieved I am that you're not the father of that baby. Now, all we need to do is let Karma know the results the next time she tries to contact you. Hopefully, she will move on."

I nodded. "So, what made you ask me about increasing our family? I told you when we got married that if you change your mind about having children, we can."

A huge smile covered her face. She went to the nightstand then pulled out a small plastic bag. She took out the content and handed it to me. It was an EPT stick. Somehow, she found time to take an Early Pregnancy Test. My mouth must've been on the floor.

"Congratulations, Daddy," she said.

"You're pregnant?" was all I could say at first. "But how? When did—" the look on her face silenced me.

"Really, Cole?"

"I mean, I know how, but when did you take this test?"

"Just now . . . when you were making sure everything was alright in the other rooms."

"Wow, sweetie. We're going to have a baby? This is great—"

Just then, our bedroom door crashed open, making a thunderous noise as it hit the wall. We jumped and turned to see a mad, screaming Karma, charging our way. She headed straight for Audrie.

"Noooooooooooo!" she screamed as she and Audrie tumbled to the floor. She wrapped her hands around Audrie's neck and squeezed. "You will NOT have my man's baby!"

I pulled on Karma, but the harder I pulled, the more her hands seemed to clamp onto Audrie's neck. Audrie's eyes were fixed on me. I could see she couldn't breathe. Her eyes were red and large veins began to reveal in her face. I knew I had to do something.

I went to the nightstand and yanked the lamp, cord and all out of the socket, then went back over toward Karma. As I lifted lamp over my head, Karma saw me then jumped up before I hit her. I heard Audrie coughing. I glanced over at her. That's when Karma kicked me between my legs, only missing my groin by inches. The kick was hard enough to take me down. The lamp flew out of my hands, hitting the wall. It was far from my reach.

"How could you do this to me?" Karma screamed as she stood over me. "I loved you, Cole! It was bad enough that you married her, but you got her pregnant, too?"

I slid away from her. "Karma," I said, coughing. "Wait. You need —"

"Don't tell me what I need! I needed you! But, you won't be here for me. So, like everybody else who has done me wrong, you have to die."

Karma scurried toward the lamp then picked it up. She started toward me. My mind ran a million miles per minute. I had to muster some strength to get up from there before she used that lamp to beat my skull in. When she raised the lamp, Audrie called her name.

"Karma!" Audrie yelled.

Karma turned to Audrie. Her eyes widened and her mouth flew open. That look on her face forced my eyes to follow hers. To my surprise, Audrie aimed a 357 Magnum at Karma. Before another sound could be made, Audrie fired one shot. BOOM. I watched Karma fall to the floor in what seemed like slow motion. The lamp fell with her, and this time, it broke into several pieces. I crawled over Karma and went to my wife. She sat, holding her chest and crying. I glanced at Karma. She was down for good. I squeezed Audrie tight and whispered in her ear.

"Sshh, it's going to be okay." I took the gun from her. "Everything is fine now."

"I knew I would have to do it," Audrie cried. "I knew it would come to this."

I set the gun beside me. "Where did you get this?"

"My sister loaned it to me. It used to be my daddy's." She looked at Karma's still body and cried some more. "I couldn't let her hurt us." She squeezed me tight.

I rocked her in my arms. "Sshh. It's okay."

Sirens filled the atmosphere. Either the police were already outside or the neighbors heard the gun shot and called 9-1-1. I heard the police beating on the front door, but I just couldn't let go of my wife. We held on to each other as they broke down our front door and entered our home. Audrie buried her head into my shoulder. The officer I'd seen cruising outside our home entered our room and walked over to Karma's body.

"Is this her?" he asked.

I nodded. I turned to Audrie. "It's over now, sweetie. Everything is going to be alright."

She squeezed me tighter, and the sense of relief she had earlier was now present with me. We both knew we could reclaim our lives.

Epilogue

(Two months later)

*E*verybody around me claimed to be hot. Some moaned. Some cried. Some even screamed, but others hardly broke a sweat. I was officially in hell. No, not literally, but sometimes it seemed like it. While everyone claimed to be hot, I was always cold. The plain, light-blue uniforms did nothing to keep me warm. This facility was much worse than the one I was once locked in. All luxuries and the freedom I once had were taken from me.

Though I was committed to another asylum, it felt more like I was in prison. I had no idea what I'd be losing if I was ever captured. This place put us on a strict diet and exercise regimen. I was made to stay in my room more often than not, and my main source of entertainment was my art pad and Crayola crayons, which were given to me by the medical staff. I longed for the old mental establishment, but my attorney said I was too much of a threat to be taken to the former hospital. That made me laugh. Me—a threat. Well, I did set the place on fire. But, nobody got hurt.

I lay in my room, massaging the shoulder Audrie shot me in. At times, it was very stiff and sore, and this was one of those times. The bitch had good aim, but not that good. I was told at the hospital that if the bullet had hit me a little more to the left, I might not be here. Audrie could've hit an artery, and I would've bled to death. Instead, I was still in a sling eight hours a day, and exercising my shoulder in half-hour increments during the rest of the day. I can still remember the day I entered Cole's home. I never figured either one of them might have a gun. Had I thought of it, I would've been more prepared. Now that I've been contained, I guess they're free to have their new baby and live happily ever after.

I searched my pack of crayons. I needed a peach color, but there wasn't one. The package only contained primary colors, which made it difficult to complete the contrast I wanted on my artwork. The door opened, distracting me. It was time for my visit to the psychiatrist's office. Before I could be walked out of my room, my hands were bound in front of me, and my ankles were secured so that I could only make small steps. This sucked. I made sure to take my art pad.

The trip to the psychiatrist's office took me about ten minutes, given the restraints on my ankles. Once inside his office, I sat in the cozy recliner next to the small sofa. The security officers and the medical assistants left the room. Dr. Weisman slid his chair from his desk then walked over to the chair in front of me.

He stood about six-two and had a lean frame with a smooth, flawless, caramel complexion. He took his seat then glanced at me.

"Good afternoon, Karma."

"Doctor." I rolled my eyes because although his voice was warm, I knew he was about to say some things that would piss me off before the meeting would be over.

He began writing something on his notepad. "Have you adjusted to your living quarters?" he asked without looking up. "Last time we spoke, you were not comfortable."

"And I'm still not comfortable. You know, Doc, you really need to tell these people how unfair they're being. It's cold all over this building, and they know it."

"Karma, no one else is complaining. I really think it's all in your mind." He tapped his bottom lip with his ink pen, reeling my attention to his neatly trimmed goatee.

I regained focus. "Here we go with the in-the-mind stuff. Listen, Doc, I'm aware you think I have a mental problem, but don't you think I would still know when I'm hot or cold?"

"That depends, Karma."

"Depends on what?"

"Have you been taking your meds? I've been told you're not very cooperative at pill time."

"No. Pills and me . . . we don't get along."

"And why not?"

"First of all, they're hard to swallow. And second of all, there isn't a pill in the world that will make me better. I'm not ill. If I'm not sick, then how is it you think a pill will do anything for me?"

"Well, Karma, I'd say you've done some things that would label you as unwell."

I gasped. "Like what?"

"The arson at your former hospital—"

"They had insurance," I snapped.

"Assuming Ms. Tyler's identity and hurting her—"

"She'll be alright."

"She doesn't remember much about who she is—"

"She's living, isn't she?" I smirked.

He sighed then jotted something before he continued. "What about the kidnapping and rape of NBA Player, Tremaine Bowman—"

"He was in good hands. Hell, he enjoyed it."

"You severed his penis—"

"He was found in time, and a surgeon put it back on."

"Karma—"

"Am I lying? I mean, that's what I heard while I was at The Criminal Justice Center, before I was brought here. He better be glad his wife tracked his phone and found him—lucky him, right?"

I laughed, but Dr. Weisman didn't seem to find it funny. "Karma, you could've killed him."

"Wouldn't've been the first time I've killed a man."

Dr. Weisman stared momentarily, and then he wrote something on his notepad. Once he finished, he looked at me, tapping his pen on his lips—again. I didn't remember his goatee having a hint of gray in it last time, but he was still good-looking. He squinted then asked, "Do you have any regrets?"

"About the killings?"

"Yes. About the murders. Do you wish you could go back and change the hands of time?"

I took a moment to think about his question. Fifteen seconds was ample time. The answer was no. If I hadn't killed my mother and stepfather, I wouldn't have moved to Memphis, and if I hadn't moved to Memphis, I wouldn't have met Cole. The others were just casualties during my fight to get Cole's attention. Perhaps if they had been in other places, they wouldn't have been victims, especially Nick. *Nick,* I thought. My attorney notified me that Nick's parents were tested, and it turned out he was Colbia's father. Had I known I was pregnant, and by Nick, I might not have killed him—but other than that, nope. I had no regrets.

Dr. Weisman seemed to be waiting on my answer as he stared at me blankly. I offered a warm smiled.

"Nope. None at all," I said, leaving out my thoughts about Nick.

Dr. Weisman was silent for a moment. Then, he said, "Do you still think of Colby?"

"Not as much as I used to."

"Oh? And why is that? Are you angry with him?"

"No. Not angry. I'm disappointed in him, but I still love him. It's just hard to think of him when there's someone else in my life?"

Dr. Weisman's eyebrows rose. "Really? So, you think you're in love again?"

"Very much so. And he loves me, too, but he hasn't admitted it."

"Does he visit you?"

"Oh, I get to see him all the time. I drew some pictures of him." I glanced at my art pad.

"May I see them?"

"Sure."

I leaned forward and stretched my art pad toward the doctor. He met me halfway then sat back in his chair. He flipped the first page and cocked his head and looked at it sideways. He flipped to the next picture, and then the next picture, and the next. His eyes slowly rose to meet mine.

"Security," he yelled, quickly standing, and then bolting toward the door. "Security!"

I laughed uncontrollably as the guards and medical staff rushed in. "Is everything alright, Dr. Weisman?" an officer asked.

Dr. Weisman stood near the door. He glanced at me. I couldn't stop laughing. "Um, yes," he answered softly. "Everything is fine. This session is over."

I was helped from my seat by the officers, and then led toward the door. I locked eyes with the doctor momentarily as I passed him.

"See you next visit, Doc," I said, grinning.

He didn't respond with his mouth, but his eyes said everything I wanted them to say. He loved me, too. He just couldn't say it right then. I knew my drawings would amaze him. He caught on fast. Maybe it was the goatee and the white doctor's coat on the man in my drawings that gave it away. Surely, he was turned on by the sight of the naked woman, kneeling with his penis in her mouth. I did my best to make the woman look like me, but there was only so much detail I could create with my crayons. But at least he got the picture—literally. He held my art pad at his side as I exited the office.

I gave him something to think about. By morning, I would ask the medical staff for another art pad. I had another picture in mind to draw that he would find more interesting than the others. I snickered at the thought of what the next drawing would do to Dr. Weisman—or, should I say Lawrence? After all, he was my new man, so it was time to be on first name bases. He was already using my first name. Security fussed as I laughed.

"Hold it down, Karma," the female officer commanded as we headed down the hall.

I calmed down—on the outside, but on the inside, I continued to giggle. It's such a joy to be in love.

Discussion Questions

1. Did Cole overreact to Audrie's paranoia? How should have he responded to his wife's concerns?

2. Was Audrie crazy for giving her marriage another chance after Cole went back to the strip club?

3. In what ways did Cole jeopardize his family's safety?

4. What did you think of Tremaine? How do you feel about what happened to him in the hotel?

5. Which of Karma's actions were extreme?

6. Should Tremaine's wife forgive him and stay?

7. Which characters surprised you, and why?

8. Did you predict the paternity results?

9. How did you feel about the consequences Karma faced in the last chapter?

10. Based on the epilogue, can you determine how the rest of Karma's story would go?

Acknowledgments

To God, I give all the Glory!

Much love to my daughters, Ebony and Imani.

Thank you to my loving and supporting parents, Rhonda and Charles Brown, Bobbie and Donald Smith, and much love to my siblings, Gregory, Ronald, Donna, and Bryant for your love and support.

Much love and thanks to Darrell Scurlock, Mary Flucker, Mindex-Mid, and to all those who love and support my work—thank you! I truly appreciate everyone who has been a part of my success and my literary endeavors.

About the Author

Playwright, Screenwriter, and National Bestselling Author, Alisha Yvonne is a native Memphian. She is the Essence® Bestselling Author of *Lovin' You Is Wrong* and *I Don't Wanna Be Right*. She is also nationally known for *Naughty Girls, The CleanUp Woman, Who's Fooling Who and* for having contributed to the bestseller, *Around the Way Girls-3*.

Alisha continues to be prolific as she ventures into the nonfiction and young adult arenas. Look for her *Hopeland High* novels, *If I Were A Boy* and *Soulja Girl*. She is currently working on her next book.

Visit Alisha online at www.alishayvonneonline.com or email to: alisha@ebonyliterarygrace.com